Praise for The Good Man Jesus and the Scoundrel Christ:

"Pullman is a supreme storyteller who . . . has done the story [of the Gospels] a service by reminding us of its extraordinary power to provoke and disturb." —*The Telegraph*

"Inspiring . . . Again and again, [Pullman] displays a marvelous sense of the elemental power of Jesus's instructions and parables. Even when he transforms the canonical stories to match his atheist perspective, he emphasizes the basic Christian theme of universal love. . . . Startling and moving. Yes, some Christians will be offended by this book . . . but any honest reader will find here a brisk and bracing story of profound implications." —*The Washington Post*

"[Philip Pullman is] one of the finest British writers of his generation. . . . The attention-grabbing title alone—*The Good Man Jesus and the Scoundrel Christ*—has been enough to rouse his enemies, and reinforce his image as a church-baiting atheist who's beyond redemption. . . . Yet this isn't the indiscriminate anger of a proselytizing atheist. Pullman is too fair-minded. . . . Love his answers or not, Pullman's honesty is hard to hate." —*Newsweek*

"Many Christian readers will recoil in horror at Mr. Pullman's plunge into heresy. But he is wrestling with the same question they are: how divinity and humanity could coexist in the founder of their religion." —*The Economist*

"Add to [Pullman's] passion his considerable gifts as a storyteller, and you have the ingredients for a powerful treatment of a familiar story. . . . He gives us an affecting portrait of faith in extremis, of a man continuing to pray even as he doubts there is any auditor to his prayers."
—*Barnes & Noble Reviews*

Also by the author

THE GOOD MAN
JESUS
AND THE
SCOUNDREL
CHRIST

PHILIP
PULLMAN

CANONGATE

Edinburgh · London · New York · Melbourne

First published in Great Britain in 2007 by Canongate Books Ltd., Edinburgh, Scotland

Portions of the afterword appeared in the *Daily Telegraph's* *Seven* magazine on April 4, 2010.

Printed in the United States of America

ISBN: 978-0-8021-4539-0

Canongate
an affiliate of Grove Atlantic
154 West 14th Street
New York, NY 10011

Distributed by Publishers Group West

groveatlantic.com

THE GOOD MAN
JESUS
AND THE
SCOUNDREL
CHRIST

Mary and Joseph

This is the story of Jesus and his brother Christ, of how they were born, of how they lived and of how one of them died. The death of the other is not part of the story.

As the world knows, their mother was called Mary. She was the daughter of Joachim and Anna, a rich, pious and elderly couple who had never had a child, much as they prayed for one. It was considered shameful that Joachim had never fathered any offspring, and he felt the shame keenly. Anna was just as unhappy. One day she saw a nest of sparrows in a laurel tree, and wept that even the birds and the beasts could produce young, when she could not.

Finally, however, possibly because of their fervent prayers, Anna conceived a child, and in due course she gave birth to a girl. Joachim and Anna vowed to dedicate her to the Lord God, so they took her to the temple and offered her to the high priest Zacharias, who kissed her and blessed her and took her into his care.

Zacharias nurtured the child like a dove, and she danced for the Lord, and everyone loved her for her grace and simplicity.

But she grew as every other girl did, and when she was twelve years old the priests of the temple realised that before long she would begin to bleed every month. That, of course, would pollute the holy place. What could they do? They had taken charge of her; they couldn't simply throw her out.

So Zacharias prayed, and an angel told him what to do. They should find a husband for Mary, but he should be a good deal older, a steady and experienced man. A widower would be ideal. The angel gave precise instructions, and promised a miracle to confirm the choice of the right man.

Accordingly, Zacharias called together as many widowers as he could find. Each one was to bring with him a wooden rod. A dozen or more men came in answer, some young, some middle-aged, some old. Among them was a carpenter called Joseph.

Consulting his instructions, Zacharias gathered all the rods together and prayed over them before giving them back. The last to receive his rod was Joseph, and as soon as it came into his hand it burst into flower.

'You're the one!' said Zacharias. 'The Lord has commanded that you should marry the girl Mary.'

'But I'm an old man!' said Joseph. 'And I have sons older than the girl. I shall be a laughing-stock.'

'Do as you are commanded,' said Zacharias, 'or face the anger of the Lord. Remember what happened to Korah.'

Korah was a Levite who had challenged the authority of Moses. As a punishment the earth opened under him and swallowed him up, together with all his household.

Joseph was afraid, and reluctantly agreed to take the girl in marriage. He took her back to his house.

'You must stay here while I go about my work,' he told her. 'I'll come back to you in good time. The Lord will watch over you.'

In Joseph's household Mary worked so hard and behaved so modestly that no one had a word of criticism for her. She spun wool, she made bread, she drew water from the well, and as she grew and became a young woman there were many who wondered at this strange marriage, and at Joseph's absence. There were others, too, young men in particular, who would try to speak to her and smile engagingly, but she said little in reply and kept her eyes on the ground. It was easy to see how simple and good she was.

And time went past.

The Birth of John

Now Zacharias the high priest was old like Joseph, and his wife Elizabeth was elderly too. Like Joachim and Anna, they had never had a child, much as they desired one.

One day Zacharias saw an angel, who told him 'Your wife will bear a child, and you must call him John.'

Zacharias was astounded, and said 'How can that possibly be? I am an old man, and my wife is barren.'

'It will happen,' said the angel. 'And until it does, you shall be mute, since you did not believe me.'

And so it was. Zacharias could no longer speak. But shortly after that Elizabeth conceived a child, and was overjoyed, because her barrenness had been a disgrace and hard to endure.

When the time came, she bore a son. As they were going to circumcise him they asked what he should be called, and Zacharias took a tablet and wrote 'John'.

His relatives were surprised, because none of the family had that name; but as soon as he had written it, Zacharias became able to speak again, and this miracle confirmed the choice. The boy was named John.

The Conception of Jesus

At that time, Mary was about sixteen years old, and Joseph had never touched her.

One night in her bedroom she heard a whisper through her window.

'Mary, do you know how beautiful you are? You are the most lovely of all women. The Lord must have favoured you especially, to be so sweet and so gracious, to have such eyes and such lips . . . '

She was confused, and said 'Who are you?'

'I am an angel,' said the voice. 'Let me in and I shall tell you a secret that only you must know.'

She opened the window and let him in. In order not to frighten her, he had assumed the appearance of a young man, just like one of the young men who spoke to her by the well.

'What is the secret?' she said.

'You are going to conceive a child,' said the angel.

Mary was bewildered.

'But my husband is away,' she said.

'Ah, the Lord wants this to happen at once. I have come from him especially to bring it about. Mary, you are blessed among women, that this should come to you! You must give thanks to the Lord.'

And that very night she conceived a child, just as the angel foretold.

When Joseph came home from the work that had taken him away, he was dismayed beyond measure to find his wife expecting a child. He hid his head in his cloak, he threw himself to the ground, he wept bitterly, he covered himself with ashes.

'Lord,' he cried, 'forgive me! Forgive me! What sort of care is this? I took this child as a virgin from the temple, and look at her now! I should have kept her safe, but I left her alone just as Adam left Eve, and look, the serpent has come to her in the same way!'

He called her to him and said 'Mary, my poor child, what have you done? You that were so pure and good, to have betrayed your innocence! Who is the man that did this?'

She wept bitterly, and said 'I've done no wrong, I swear! I have never been touched by a man! It was an angel that came to me, because God wanted me to conceive a child!'

Joseph was troubled. If this was really God's will, it must be his duty to look after her and the child. But it would look bad all the same. Nevertheless, he said no more.

The Birth of Jesus, and the Coming of the Shepherds

Not long afterwards there came a decree from the Roman emperor, saying that everyone should go to their ancestral town in order to be counted in a great census. Joseph lived in Nazareth in Galilee, but his family had come from Bethlehem in Judea, some days' journey to the south. He thought to himself: How shall I have them record Mary's name? I can list my sons, but what shall I do with her? Shall I call her my wife? I'd be ashamed. Should I call her my daughter? But people know that she's not my daughter, and besides, it's obvious that she's expecting a child. What can I do?

In the end he set off, with Mary riding a donkey behind him. The child was due to be born any day, and still Joseph did not know what he was going to say about his wife. When they had nearly reached Bethlehem, he turned around to see how she was, and saw her looking sad. Perhaps she's in pain, he thought. A little later he turned around again, and this time saw her laughing.

'What is it?' he said. 'A moment ago you were looking sad, and now you're laughing.'

'I saw two men,' she said, 'and one of them was weeping and crying, and the other was laughing and rejoicing.'

There was no one in sight. He thought: How can this be?

But he said no more, and soon they came to the town. Every inn was full, and Mary was crying and trembling, for the child was about to be born.

'There's no room,' said the last innkeeper they asked. 'But you can sleep in the stable – the beasts will keep you warm.'

Joseph spread their bedding on the straw and made Mary comfortable, and ran to find a midwife. When he came back the child was already born, but the midwife said 'There's another to come. She is having twins.'

And sure enough, a second child was born soon afterwards. They were both boys, and the first was strong and healthy, but the second was small, weak, and sickly. Mary wrapped the strong boy in cloth and laid him in the feeding trough, and suckled the other first, because she felt sorry for him.

That night there were shepherds keeping watch over their flocks on the hills outside the town. An angel appeared to them glowing with light, and the shepherds were terrified until the angel said 'Don't be afraid. Tonight a child has been born in the town, and he will be the Messiah. You will know him by this sign: you will find him wrapped in bands of cloth and lying in a feeding trough.'

The shepherds were pious Jews, and they knew what *the Messiah* meant. The prophets had foretold that the Messiah, the Anointed One, would come to rescue the Israelites from their oppression. The Jews had had many oppressors over the centuries; the latest were the Romans, who had occupied the land for some years now. Many people expected the Messiah to lead the Jewish people in battle and free them from the power of Rome.

So they set off to the town to find him. Hearing the sound of a baby's cry, they made their way to the stable beside the inn, where they found an elderly man watching over a young woman who was nursing a new-born baby. Beside them in the feeding trough lay another baby wrapped in bands of cloth, and this was the one that was crying. And it was the second child, the sickly one, because Mary had nursed him first and set him to lie down while she nursed the other.

'We have come to see the Messiah,' said the shepherds, and explained about the angel and how he had told them where to find the baby.

'This one?' said Joseph.

'That is what we were told. That is how we knew him. Who would have thought to look for a child in a feeding trough? It must be him. He must be the one sent from God.'

Mary heard this without surprise. Hadn't she been told something similar by the angel who came to her bedroom? However, she was proud and happy that her little helpless son was receiving such tribute and praise. The other didn't need it; he was strong and quiet and calm, like Joseph. One for Joseph, and one for me, thought Mary, and kept this idea in her heart, and said nothing of it.

The Astrologers

At the same time some astrologers from the East arrived in Jerusalem, looking, so they claimed, for the king of the Jews, who had just been born. They had worked this out from their observations of the planets, and calculated the child's horoscope with every detail of ascendant and transit and progression.

Naturally, they first went to the palace and asked to see the royal child. King Herod was suspicious, and called for them to come to him and explain.

'Our calculations show that a child has been born nearby who will be the king of the Jews. We assumed he had been brought to the palace, so we came here first. We have brought gifts—'

'How interesting,' said Herod. 'And where was he born, this royal child?'

'In Bethlehem.'

'Come a little closer,' said the king, lowering his voice. 'You understand – you are men of the world, you know these things – for reasons of state I have to be very careful what I say. There are powers abroad that you and I know little about, but they wouldn't hesitate to kill such a child if they found him, and the most important thing now is to protect him. You go to Bethlehem – make enquiries – and as soon as you have any information, come and tell me. I'll make sure that the dear child is looked after safely.'

So the astrologers went the few miles south to Bethlehem to find the child. They looked at their star charts, they consulted their books, they made lengthy calculations, and finally, after asking at nearly every house in Bethlehem, they found the family they were looking for.

'So this is the child who is to rule over the Jews!' they said. 'Or is it that one?'

Mary proudly held out her little weak son. The other was sleeping peacefully nearby. The astrologers paid homage to the child in his mother's arms, and opened their treasure chests and gave gifts: gold, and frankincense, and myrrh.

'You've come from Herod, you say?' said Joseph.

'Oh, yes. He wants us to go back and tell him

where to find you, so he can make sure the child is safe.'

'If I were you,' said Joseph, 'I'd go straight home. The king is unpredictable, you know. He might take it into his head to punish you. We'll take the child to him in good time, don't worry.'

The astrologers thought this was good advice, and went their way. Meanwhile, Joseph packed their goods hastily, and set off that very night with Mary and the children and went to Egypt, because he knew King Herod's volatile ways, and feared what he would do.

The Death of Zacharias

He was right to do so. When Herod realised that the astrologers were not going to come back, he flew into a rage and ordered that every child in Bethlehem and the neighbourhood under two years of age should be killed at once.

One of the children of the right age was John, the son of Zacharias and Elizabeth. As soon as they heard of Herod's plan, Elizabeth took him up into the mountains looking for somewhere to hide. But she was old and could not walk very far, and in her despair she cried out 'Oh mountain of God, shelter a mother and her child!'

At once the mountain opened and offered her a cave in which to shelter.

So she and the child were safe, but Zacharias was in trouble. Herod knew that he had recently fathered a child, and sent for him.

'Where is your child? Where have you hidden him?'

'I am a busy priest, Your Majesty! I spend all

my time about the business of the temple! Looking after children is women's work. I don't know where my son can be.'

'I warn you – tell the truth! I can spill your blood if I want to.'

'If you shed my blood, I shall be a martyr to the Lord,' said Zacharias, and that came true, because he was killed there and then.

The Childhood of Jesus

Meanwhile, Joseph and Mary were deciding what to call their sons. The firstborn was to be named Jesus, but what to call the other, Mary's secret favourite? In the end they gave him a common name, but in view of what the shepherds had said, Mary always called him Christ, which is Greek for Messiah. Jesus was a strong and cheerful baby, but Christ was often ill, and Mary worried about him, and gave him the warmest blankets, and let him suck honey from her fingertip to stop him crying.

Not long after they had arrived in Egypt, Joseph heard that King Herod had died. It was safe to go back, and so they set off to Joseph's home town of Nazareth in Galilee. There the children grew up.

And as time passed there came more children to join them, more brothers, and sisters too. Mary loved all her children, but not equally. The little Christ seemed to her to need special care. Where

Jesus and the other children were boisterous and played loudly together, getting into mischief, stealing fruit, shouting out rude names and running away, picking fights, throwing stones, daubing mud on house walls, catching sparrows, Christ clung to his mother's skirts and spent hours in reading and prayer.

One day Mary went to the house of a neighbour who was a dyer. Jesus and Christ both came with her, and while she was talking to the dyer, with Christ close by her side, Jesus went into the workshop. He looked at all the vessels containing different coloured dyes, and dipped a finger in each one, and then wiped them on the pile of cloths waiting to be dyed. Then he thought that the dyer would notice and be angry with him, so he bundled up the entire pile and thrust it all into the vessel containing a black dye.

He went back to the room where his mother was talking to the dyer, and Christ saw him and said 'Mama, Jesus has done something wrong.'

Jesus had his hands behind him.

'Show me your hands,' said Mary.

He brought his hands around to show. They were coloured black, red, yellow, purple and blue.

'What have you been doing?' she said.

Alarmed, the dyer ran into his workshop. Bulging out of the top of the vessel with the black dye was an untidy heap of cloth, besmeared and stained with black, and with other colours as well.

'Oh no! Look what this brat has done!' he cried. 'All this cloth — it'll cost me a fortune!'

'Jesus, you bad boy!' said Mary. 'Look, you've destroyed all this man's work! We'll have to pay for it. How can we do that?'

'But I thought I was helping,' said Jesus.

'Mama,' said Christ, 'I can make it all better.'

And he took a corner of cloth, and said to the dyer:

'What colour is this one supposed to be, sir?'

'Red,' said the dyer.

And the child pulled it out of the vessel, and it was red all over. Then he pulled out each of the remaining cloths, asking the dyer what colour it should be, and so they were: each piece was perfectly dyed just as the customer had ordered it.

The dyer marvelled, and Mary embraced the child Christ and kissed him again and again, filled with joy at the goodness of the little fellow.

Another time Jesus was playing beside the ford across a brook, and he made some little sparrows out of mud and set them all up in a row. A pious Jew who was passing saw what he was doing and went to tell Joseph.

'Your son has broken the sabbath!' he said. 'Do you know what he's doing down by the ford? You should control your children!'

Joseph hurried to see what Jesus was doing. Christ had heard the man shouting, and followed close behind Joseph. Other people were following too, having heard the commotion. They got there just as Jesus made the twelfth sparrow.

'Jesus!' Joseph said. 'Stop that at once. You know this is the sabbath.'

They were going to punish Jesus, but Christ clapped his hands, and at once the sparrows came alive and flew away. The people were amazed.

'I didn't want my brother to get into trouble,' Christ explained. 'He's a good boy really.'

And all the adults were filled with admiration.

The little boy was so modest and thoughtful, not a bit like his brother. But the children of the town preferred Jesus.

The Visit to Jerusalem

When the twins were twelve years old, Joseph and Mary took them to Jerusalem for the feast of the Passover. They travelled down in a company of other families, and there were many adults to keep an eye on the children. After the festival, when they were gathering everyone together to leave, Mary made sure that Christ was with her, and said to him:

'Where is Jesus? I can't see him anywhere.'

'I think he's with the family of Zachaeus,' said Christ. 'He was playing with Simon and Jude. He told me he was going to travel home with them.'

So they set off, and Mary and Joseph thought no more about him, imagining him safe with the other family. But when it was time for the evening meal, Mary sent Christ to Zachaeus's family to call Jesus, and he came back excited and anxious.

'He's not with them! He told me he was going to play with them, but he never did! They haven't seen him anywhere!'

Mary and Joseph searched among their relatives and friends, and asked every group of travellers if they had seen Jesus, but none of them knew where he was. This one said they had last seen him playing outside the temple, that one said they had heard him say he was going to the marketplace, another said they were sure he was with Thomas, or Saul, or Jacob. In the end Joseph and Mary had to accept that he had been left behind, and they packed their things away and turned back towards Jerusalem. Christ rode on the donkey, because Mary was worried that he might be tired.

They searched through the city for three days, but Jesus was nowhere to be found. Finally Christ said 'Mama, should we go to the temple and pray for him?'

Since they had looked everywhere else, they thought they would try that. And as soon as they entered the temple grounds, they heard a commotion.

'That'll be him,' said Joseph.

Sure enough, it was. The priests had found Jesus daubing his name on the wall with clay, and were deciding how to punish him.

'It's only clay!' he was saying, brushing the dirt

off his hands. 'As soon as it rains, it'll come off again! I wouldn't dream of damaging the temple. I was writing my name there in the hope that God would see it and remember me.'

'Blasphemer!' said a priest.

And he would have struck Jesus, but Christ stepped forward and spoke.

'Please, sir,' he said, 'my brother is not a blasphemer. He was writing his name in clay so as to express the words of Job, "Remember that you fashioned me like clay; and will you turn me to dust again?"'

'That may be,' said another, 'but he knows full well he's done wrong. Look – he's tried to wash his hands and conceal the evidence.'

'Well, of course he has,' said Christ. 'He has done it to fulfil the words of Jeremiah, "Though you wash yourself with lye and use much soap, the stain of your guilt is still before you."'

'But to run away from your family!' Mary said to Jesus. 'We've been terrified! Anything could have happened to you. But you're so selfish, you don't know what it means to think of others. Your family means nothing to you!'

Jesus hung his head. But Christ said:

'No, Mama, I'm sure he means well. And this too was foretold. He's done this so that the psalm can come true, "I have borne reproach, and shame has covered my face. I have become a stranger to my kindred, an alien to my mother's children."'

The priests and teachers of the temple were amazed at the knowledge of the little Christ, and praised his learning and quickness of mind. Since he had pleaded so well, they allowed Jesus to go unpunished.

But on the way back to Nazareth, Joseph said privately to Jesus 'What were you thinking of, to upset your mother like that? You know how tender-hearted she is. She was worried sick about you.'

'And you, Father, were you worried?'

'I was worried for her, and I was worried for you.'

'You didn't need to worry for me. I was safe enough.'

Joseph said no more.

The Coming of John

Time went past, and the two boys grew to manhood. Jesus learned the trade of carpentry, and Christ spent all his time in the synagogue, reading the scriptures and discussing their meanings with the teachers. Jesus took no notice of Christ, but for his part, Christ was always forbearing, and keen to display a friendly interest in his brother's work.

'We need carpenters,' he would say earnestly. 'It's a fine trade. Jesus is coming on very well. He will be able to marry one day soon, I'm sure. He deserves a good wife and a home.'

By this time the man John, the son of Zacharias and Elizabeth, had begun a campaign of preaching in the country around the Jordan, impressing the people with his teaching about the need for repentance and with his promise of the forgiveness of sins. There were many wandering preachers in Galilee and the surrounding districts at that time; some were good men, some were wicked charlatans, and some were simply mad. John was unusual in his simplicity and directness. He had spent some time in the wilderness, and dressed roughly and ate little. He invented the rite of baptism to symbolise the washing-away of sin, and many came to listen to him and to be baptised.

Among the people who came to listen to him were some Sadducees and Pharisees. These were two rival groups among the Jewish teachers. They disagreed with one another about many matters of doctrine, but each was important and influential.

John, however, treated them with scorn.

'You brood of vipers! Running away from the anger to come, are you? You'd do better to start doing some good in the world, better to start bearing some fruit. The axe is already lying at the root of the trees. Watch out, because it will cut down every tree that doesn't bear good fruit, and they will be thrown on the fire.'

'But what should we do to be good?' people asked him.

'If you have two coats, give one to someone who has none. If you have more food than you need, share it with someone who is hungry.'

Even some tax-collectors came for baptism.

Tax-collectors were hated by the people, because everyone resented paying money to the occupying forces of Rome. But John didn't turn them away.

'What must we do, teacher?' said the tax-collectors.

'Take in exactly as much tax as you should, and not a penny more.'

Some soldiers came to him too.

'Will you baptise us? Tell us what we must do to be good!'

'Be content with your regular wages, and don't extort money from anyone with threats or false accusations.'

John became famous in the countryside for the vigour of his words as well as for the ceremony of baptism. He had recently said something that was widely spoken about:

'I baptise you with water, but there's someone else coming who is much more powerful than I am. I'm not worthy to untie his sandals for him. He will baptise you with the Holy Spirit and with fire. He's going to sort the wheat from the chaff; he's got his winnowing-fork in his hand already; the grain will be safe in the granary, but the chaff will burn with a fire that never goes out.'

The Baptism of Jesus

Word of his teaching came to Nazareth, and Jesus was curious to go and listen to him. He set off for the Jordan, where he heard that John was preaching. Christ went as well, but the two brothers travelled separately. When they reached the river bank they joined the crowd waiting to be immersed in the water, and watched as the people went down one by one to join the Baptist where he stood waist-deep, wearing the rough camel-hair cloak that was his only garment.

When it was Jesus's turn, John held up his hand in refusal.

'It should be you who baptise me,' he said.

Christ, watching from the bank as he waited for his turn, heard his words with astonishment.

'No,' replied Jesus, 'I've come to you. Just do it in the proper way.'

So John held him, and plunged him under the water and lifted him up again.

At that moment Christ saw a dove fly above

them and settle in a tree. It might have been an omen. Christ wondered what it might mean, and imagined what a voice might say if it spoke from heaven and told him.

The Temptation of Jesus
in the Wilderness

After the baptism Jesus and Christ listened to the
preaching of John, and it made a great impression
on them both. In fact, Jesus was so impressed by
the personality and the words of the Baptist that
he decided to give up his trade of carpentry and
go into the wilderness as John had done, and see
if he too could hear the words of God. So he went
off on his own into the desert, wandering from
place to place, eating little and sleeping on the
rough ground.

Meanwhile Christ went home to Nazareth, and
told Mary about the baptism, and told her about
the dove, too.

'It flew right over my head, Mother. And I
thought I heard a voice speaking from heaven. It
was the voice of God, and it was speaking to me
– I'm sure of it.'

'Of course it was, darling! It was your special
baptism.'

'Do you think I should go and tell Jesus?'

'If you want to, dear. If you think he'll listen.'

So he set off, and forty days after Jesus had gone into the wilderness, Christ found him kneeling in a dry river bed and praying. He watched and waited, thinking of what to say, and when Jesus stopped and lay down in the shade of a rock, Christ came and spoke to him.

'Jesus, have you heard the word of God yet?'

'Why do you want to know?'

'Because something happened when you were being baptised. I saw the heavens open above you, and a dove come down and hovered above your head, and a voice said "This is my beloved son".'

Jesus said nothing. Christ said:

'Don't you believe me?'

'No. Of course not.'

'It's plain that God has chosen you for something special. Look what the Baptist himself said to you.'

'He was mistaken.'

'No, I'm sure he wasn't. You're popular, people like you, they listen to what you say. You're a good man. You're passionate and impulsive, and those are fine qualities, of course they are, as long as they're regulated by custom and authority. You could have a lot of influence. It would be a shame not to use it for good. The Baptist would agree with me, I know.'

'Go away.'

'I know what it is, you're tired and hungry after all this time in the desert. If you're the son of God, as I heard the voice say, you could command these stones to become loaves of bread, and they'd have to, and then you could eat as much as you wanted.'

'Oh, you think so? I know the scriptures, you scoundrel. "Man does not live by bread alone, but by every word that comes from the mouth of God." Had you forgotten that? Or did you think I had?'

'Of course I don't think you've forgotten your lessons,' said Christ. 'You were as clever as anyone in the class. But consider what good you could do if you could feed the hungry! If they ask for food, you could give them a stone and it would become bread! Think of the starving, think of the misery of famine, think of the bitterness of poverty and the dread of a poor harvest! And you need food just as the poor do. If you're to do the work that

God obviously wants you to do, you can't do it hungry.'

'It didn't occur to you to bring me a loaf yourself, I notice. That would have been more use than a sermon.'

'There's bodily food, and there's spiritual food—' began Christ, but Jesus threw a stone at him, and he retreated a little way.

Presently he spoke again.

'Jesus, don't be angry with me. Just hear me out. I know you want to do good, I know you want to help people. I know you want to do the will of God. But you must consider the effect you could have – the effect on ordinary people, simple people, ignorant people. They can be led to the good, but they need signs and wonders. They need miracles. Fine words convince the mind, but miracles speak directly to the heart and then to the soul. Don't despise the very means that God has placed in our nature. If a simple person sees stones changed into bread, or sees sick people healed, this makes an impression on him that could change his life. He'll believe every word you say from then on. He'll follow you to the ends of the earth.'

'You think the word of God can be conveyed by conjuring tricks?'

'That's a harsh way of putting it. Miracles have always been part of God's way of convincing his people. Think of Moses leading his people through the Red Sea. Think of Elijah reviving the widow's son. Think of the poor woman whose creditors were demanding payment, and Elisha telling her to pour her one jar of oil into several empty ones, and they were all filled, so she could sell them and pay her debts. By showing people miracles like this, we bring them face to face with the infinite power of God's goodness, and we do it with vivid immediacy, so their simple hearts see and understand and believe at once.'

'You keep saying "we",' said Jesus. 'Are you one of these miracle-workers, then?'

'Not just me alone, but you and me together!'

'Never.'

'But think of what an effect it would have if someone were to go to the top of the temple, say, and to step off into the air, full of faith that God would do what it says in the psalms, and send his angels to catch him. "He has commanded his angels to guard you wherever you go, and they will hold you in their arms so that you will not dash your foot against a stone." Just imagine—'

'Is that all you've learned from the scriptures? To put on a sensational show for the credulous? You'd do better to forget about that and attend to the real meaning of things. Remember what the scripture says: "Do not put the Lord your God to the test."'

'What is the real meaning of things, then?'

'God loves us like a father, and his Kingdom is coming soon.'

Christ came a little closer.

'But that's exactly what we can demonstrate with miracles,' he said. 'And the Kingdom is a test for us, I'm sure: we must help to bring it about. Of course, God could lift a finger and it would happen at once. But think how much better it would be if the way were prepared by men like the Baptist, men like you – think of the advantages if there were a body of believers, a structure, an organisation already in place. I can see it so clearly, Jesus! I can see the whole world united in this Kingdom of the faithful – think of that! Groups of families worshipping together with a priest in every village and town, an association of local groups under the direction and guidance of a wise elder in the region, the regional leaders all answering to the authority of one supreme director, a kind of regent of God on earth! And there would be councils of learned men to discuss and agree on the details of ritual and worship, and even more importantly, to rule on the intricacies of faith, to declare what was to be believed and what was to be shunned. I can see the princes of the nations – I can see Caesar himself having to bow down before this body, and offer obeisance to God's own Kingdom in place here in the world. And I can see the laws and the proclamations issuing from the centre to the furthest edges of the world. I can see the good rewarded and the wicked punished. I can see missionaries going out bearing the word of God to the darkest and most ignorant lands, and bringing every living man and woman and child into the great family of God – yes, Gentiles as well as Jews. I can see all doubt vanquished, I can see all dissent swept away, I can see the shining faces of the faithful gazing up in adoration on every side. I can see the majesty and the splendour of the great temples, the courts, the palaces devoted to the glory of God, and I can see

this whole wonderful creation lasting for generation after generation and for thousand years after
thousand years! Isn't this a vision worth marvel-
ling at, Jesus? Isn't this something to work for with
every drop of blood in our bodies? Won't you join
me in this? Won't you be a part of this most
wonderful work and help bring the Kingdom of
God to earth?'

Jesus looked at his brother.

'You phantom,' he said, 'you shadow of a man.
Every drop of blood in our bodies? You have no
blood to speak of; it would be my blood that you'd
offer up to this vision of yours. What you describe
sounds like the work of Satan. God will bring
about his Kingdom in his own way, and when he
chooses. Do you think your mighty organisation
would even recognise the Kingdom if it arrived?
Fool! The Kingdom of God would come into
these magnificent courts and palaces like a poor
traveller with dust on his feet. The guards would
spot him at once, ask for his papers, beat him,
throw him out into the street. "Be on your way,"
they'd say, "you have no business here."'

'I'm sorry you see it like that,' said Christ.
'But I wish you'd let me persuade you otherwise.

It's exactly that passion, that impeccable moral sense, that purity of yours that would be so useful. I know we'll get some things wrong to start with. Won't you come and help get them right? There's no one alive who could guide us better than you. Isn't it better to compromise a little, to come inside and improve something, than to stay on the outside and offer nothing but criticism?'

'One day someone will say those words to you, and your belly will convulse with sickness and shame. Now leave me alone. Worship God – that's the only task you need to think about.'

Christ left Jesus in the wilderness, and went home to Nazareth.

Joseph Greets his Son

Joseph was very old by this time, and when he saw Christ coming into the house he mistook him for his firstborn, and struggled to his feet to embrace him.

'Jesus!' he said. 'My dear boy! Where have you been? I've missed you so much! It was bad of you to go away like that without telling me.'

Christ said 'It's not Jesus, Father, it's me, your son Christ.'

Joseph stood back and said 'But where is Jesus? I miss him. I think it's a shame that he's not here. Why did he go away?'

'He is in the wilderness, doing what he wants to do,' said Christ.

Joseph was saddened, because he thought he might never see Jesus again. The wilderness was full of dangers; anything could happen there.

But a little later Joseph heard a rumour in the town that Jesus had been seen on his way home, and he ordered a great feast to be prepared to celebrate his homecoming. Christ was in the synagogue when he heard about this, and he hurried out and reproached his father.

'Father, why are you preparing a feast for Jesus? I have been at home all the time, I've never disobeyed your commands, and yet you've never prepared a feast for me. Jesus walked away with no warning, he left you with work to do, he has no thought for his family or anyone else.'

'Well, you're at home all the time,' said Joseph. 'All that I have is yours. But when someone comes home after being away, it's right and proper to prepare a feast in celebration.'

And when Jesus was still some way off, Joseph hurried out to greet him. He embraced him and kissed him warmly. Jesus was moved by the old man's gesture, and said 'Father, I've sinned against you; it was wrong of me to go away without telling you. I don't deserve to be called your son.'

'My dear son! I thought you were dead, and here you are, alive!'

And Joseph kissed him again, and put a clean robe around his shoulders and led him in to the feast. Christ greeted his brother warmly, but

Jesus looked at him as if he knew just what Christ had said to his father. No one else had heard it, and no one saw the look that passed between them.

Jesus Begins his Ministry

Not long afterwards came news that John the Baptist had been arrested by order of King Herod Antipas, the son of the Herod who had ordered the massacre of the children in Bethlehem. The king had taken away the wife of his brother Philip and married her, in defiance of the law of Moses, and John had criticised him boldly. The king was angry, and ordered his arrest.

That seemed to be a signal for Jesus, and he began at once to preach and teach in Capernaum and the nearby towns around the Sea of Galilee. Like John, he warned people to repent of their sins, and told them that the Kingdom of God was very near and would be coming soon. Many people were impressed by his words, but some thought he was reckless, because the Roman authorities would not be pleased to hear such inflammatory words, and neither would the leaders of the Jews.

And soon Jesus began to attract followers. As

he was walking along the shore of the lake one day he fell into conversation with two brothers, fishermen called Peter and Andrew, who were casting a net into the water.

'Come with me,' he said, 'and help me catch men and women instead of fish.'

Seeing these two go with him, some other fishermen called James and John, the sons of Zebedee, left their father and followed him too.

Before long Jesus was renowned in the district not only for his words but also for the remarkable events that were said to happen wherever he was. For example, he went to Peter's house one day, and found Peter's mother-in-law sick with a fever. Jesus went in to speak to her, and presently she felt well again and got up to serve them all food. This was said to be a miracle.

Another time, he was in the synagogue at Capernaum on the Sabbath, when a man began shouting 'Why have you come here, Jesus of Nazareth? What d'you think you're doing? Leave us alone! Have you come to destroy us? I know who you are! You call yourself the Holy One of God – is that who you are? Is it?'

The man was a harmless obsessive, one of

those poor creatures who shout and scream for reasons even they don't understand, and hear voices and talk to people who aren't there.

Jesus looked at him calmly and said 'You can be quiet now. He's gone away.'

The man fell silent and stood there abashed, as if he had just woken up to find himself in the middle of the crowd. After that he cried out no more, and people said that it was because Jesus had exorcised him and driven away a devil. So the stories began to spread. People said he could cure all kinds of diseases, and that evil spirits fled when he spoke.

When he returned to Nazareth he went to the synagogue on the sabbath, as he always did. He stood up to read, and the attendant handed him the scroll of the prophet Isaiah.

'Isn't this the son of Joseph the carpenter?' someone whispered.

'I hear he's been preaching around Capernaum, and working miracles,' whispered someone else.

'If he's from Nazareth, why does he go and perform miracles in Capernaum?' whispered another. 'He'd do better to stay here and do some good in his home town.'

Jesus read the words from one part of the book and from another:

'The spirit of the Lord is upon me, because he has anointed me to bring good news to the poor.

'He has sent me to proclaim release to the captives and recovery of sight to the blind, to let the oppressed go free,

'To proclaim the year of the Lord's favour.'

He gave the scroll back. All eyes were fixed on him, because everyone was eager to hear what he would say.

'You want a prophet,' he said. 'More than that: you want a miracle-worker. I heard the whispers that ran around the synagogue when I stood up. You want me to do here the things you've heard about from Capernaum – well, I've heard those rumours too, and I have more sense than to believe them. You need to think a bit harder. Some of you know who I am: Jesus, the son of Joseph the carpenter, and this is my home town. When has a prophet ever been honoured in his home town? Consider this, if you think you deserve miracles because of who you are: when there was a famine in the land of Israel, and no rain fell for three years, whom did the prophet Elijah help, by God's command? An Israelite widow? No, a widow from Zarephath in Sidon. A foreigner. And again, were there lepers in the land of Israel in Elisha's time? There were many. And whom did he cure? Naaman the Syrian. You think being what you *are* is enough? You'd better start considering what you *do*.'

Christ was listening to every word his brother spoke, and watching the people carefully, and he wasn't surprised when a great wave of anger rose among them. He knew these words would provoke them; it was exactly what he would have warned Jesus about, if he'd been asked. This was no way to get a message across.

'Who does this man think he is?' said one.

'How dare he come here and speak to us like this!' said another.

'This is scandalous!' said a third. 'We shouldn't have to listen to this man running down his own people, right here in the synagogue!'

And before Jesus could say any more they rose to their feet and seized him. They dragged him to the hill above the town, and they would have hurled him from the top; but in the confusion and the struggle – for some of Jesus's friends and followers were there too, and they fought the townspeople – Jesus managed to get away unharmed.

But Christ had watched it all, and considered the significance of what he'd seen. Wherever Jesus went there was excitement, enthusiasm, and danger too. It surely wouldn't be long before the authorities took an interest.

The Stranger

Now at about that time a stranger came to Christ and spoke to him privately.

'I'm interested in you,' he said. 'Your brother is attracting all the attention, but I think you are the one I should speak to.'

'Who are you?' said Christ. 'And how do you know about me? I have never spoken in public, unlike Jesus.'

'I heard a story about your birth. Some shepherds saw a vision that led them to you, and some magicians from the East brought you gifts. Isn't that so?'

'Why, yes,' said Christ.

'And I spoke to your mother yesterday, and she told me of what happened when John baptised Jesus. You heard a voice speaking from a cloud.'

'My mother should not have spoken of that,' said Christ modestly.

'And some years ago, you confounded the priests in the temple at Jerusalem when your brother got into trouble. People remember these things.'

'But – who are you? And what do you want?'

'I want to make sure that you have your rightful reward. I want the world to know your name as well as that of Jesus. In fact I want your name to shine with even greater splendour. He is a man, and only a man, but you are the word of God.'

'I don't know that expression, the word of God. What does it mean? And again, sir – who are you?'

'There is time, and there is what is beyond time. There is darkness, and there is light. There is the world and the flesh, and there is God. These things are separated by a gulf deeper than any man can measure, and no man can cross it; but the word of God can come from God to the world and the flesh, from light to darkness, from what is beyond time into time. Now I must go away, and you must watch and wait, but I shall come to you again.'

And he left. Christ had not found out his name, but the stranger had spoken with such knowledge and clarity that Christ knew, without having to

ask, that he was an important teacher, no doubt
a priest, perhaps from Jerusalem itself. After all,
he had mentioned the incident in the temple, and
how else would he have heard about it?

Jesus and the Wine

After being thrown out of the synagogue at Nazareth, Jesus found crowds following wherever he went. Some people said that his words showed he had gone out of his mind, and his family tried to speak to him and restrain him, for they were worried about what he would do.

But he took little notice of his family. Once, at a wedding in the village of Cana, his mother said to him 'Jesus, they've run out of wine.'

Jesus answered 'What's that got to do with me, or with you? Are you like my brother, that you want me to perform a miracle?'

Mary did not know how to answer that, so she simply said to the servants 'Just do as he says.'

Jesus took the chief steward aside and spoke to him, and soon afterwards the servants discovered more wine. Some said Jesus had created it out of water by means of magic, but others said that the steward had hidden it, hoping to sell it, and Jesus had shamed him into honesty; and yet others only remembered the rough way Jesus spoke to his mother.

Another time, when he was speaking to a group of strangers, someone came and told him 'Your mother and your brothers and sisters are outside, asking for you.'

Jesus replied: 'My mother and my brothers and sisters are right here in front of me. I have no family except those who do the will of God, and whoever does the will of God is my mother and my brother and my sister.'

Word of that got back to his family, and they were dismayed. That only added to the scandal that was beginning to surround his name, of course, and gave the people something else to spread stories about.

Jesus was aware of the way people were talking about him, and he tried to discourage it. Once, a man whose skin was covered in boils and running sores came to him privately, and said 'Lord, if you choose to, you can cure my disease.'

The usual ritual for cleansing a leper (as those with skin diseases were commonly called) was lengthy and expensive. This man might simply have been trying to avoid the cost, but Jesus saw the trust in his eyes, and reached out to embrace him, and kissed his face. And at once the man felt better. Christ, who was nearby, was the only person who was watching, and he saw Jesus's gesture with astonishment.

'Now go to the priest, as Moses commanded,' Jesus told the leper, 'and get a certificate of cleanliness. But say nothing about this to anyone else, you hear me?'

However, the man disobeyed him and spoke about his cure to everyone he met. Naturally, this made Jesus even more in demand, and wherever he went people came to him both to hear his preaching and to be cured of their sicknesses.

Jesus Scandalises the Scribes

The local teachers and religious lawyers, the scribes, who were alarmed by his fame, thought they should take steps to deal with him, so they began to attend whenever Jesus was teaching. On one occasion the house where he was speaking was crowded, and some men who had carried a paralysed friend there in the hope that Jesus would heal him found they could not get in at the door; so they carried him up to the roof, scraped off the plaster, removed the beams, and lowered the sick man on a mat down in front of him.

Jesus saw that the man and his friends had come in honest hope and faith, and that the crowd was excited and tense with expectation. Knowing the effect it would have, he said to the paralysed man 'Friend, your sins are forgiven.'

The scribes – village lawyers most of them, men of no great skill or learning – said to one another 'This is blasphemy! Only God can forgive sins. This man is asking for trouble!'

Jesus saw them whisper, and knew what they would be saying, so he challenged them.

'Why don't you come out with it?' he said. 'Tell me this: which is easier, to say "Your sins are forgiven", or to say "Take up your mat and walk"?'

The scribes fell into the trap he'd set, and said 'To say "Your sins are forgiven", of course.'

'Very well,' said Jesus, and turning to the paralysed man, he said 'Now, take up your mat and walk.'

The man was so strengthened and inspired by the atmosphere Jesus had created that he found himself able to move. He did just what Jesus had told him to do: he got to his feet, picked up his mat, and went to join his friends outside. The people were scarcely able to believe what they'd seen, and the scribes were confounded.

Soon after that, they had something else to be scandalised about. Jesus was walking past a tax office one day, and he stopped to talk to the tax-collector, who was a man called Matthew. Just as he'd done to the fishermen Peter and Andrew, and to James and John the sons of Zebedee, Jesus said to Matthew 'Come and follow me.'

At once Matthew left his coins, his abacus, his

files and records, and stood up to go with Jesus. In order to mark his new calling as a follower, he gave a dinner for Jesus and the other disciples, and invited many of his old colleagues from the tax department. That was the scandal: the scribes who heard about it could hardly believe that a Jewish teacher, a man who spoke in the synagogue, would share a meal with tax-collectors.

'Why is he doing this?' they said to some of the disciples. 'We have to speak with these people from time to time, but to sit and eat with them!'

Jesus didn't find that charge difficult to answer. 'Those who are not sick need no doctor,' he said. 'And there's no need to call righteous people to repent. To speak with sinners is exactly why I've come.'

Naturally, Christ was following all this with great interest. Obeying the stranger's instruction to watch and wait, he was careful not to draw any attention to himself, but stayed in Nazareth, living quietly. He didn't find that hard to do; although he resembled his brother, of course, he had the sort of face that few people remember, and his manner was always modest and retiring.

Nevertheless, he took care to listen to all the

reports that came back to the family about what Jesus was doing. It was a time when political feeling in Galilee was beginning to stir; groups such as the Zealots were urging the Jews to active resistance against the Romans, and Christ was anxious in case his brother should attract the wrong sort of attention, and become a target of the authorities.

And he waited every day in hope of meeting the stranger again, and hearing more about his task as the word of God.

Jesus Preaches on the Mountain

One day Jesus went out to find a great crowd of people who had come from far away: as well as those from Galilee, people had come from the lands of the Decapolis beyond the Jordan, from Jerusalem and Judea. In order to make it easier for them all to hear his teaching, Jesus climbed up into the mountains a little way, with his disciples and the crowd following. Christ was inconspicuous among them, and no one knew who he was, for they were all strangers to the district. He had a tablet and a stylus with him to take notes about what Jesus said.

When Jesus had reached a prominent spot, he began to speak.

'What am I preaching?' he said. 'The Kingdom of God, that's what. It's coming, friends, it's on its way. And today I'm going to tell you who's going to be received into the Kingdom, and who isn't, so pay attention. It's the difference between being blessed and being cursed. Don't ignore what I say to you, now. A great deal hangs on this.

'So here you are then: the poor will be blessed. Those who have nothing now will soon inherit all the Kingdom of God.

'The hungry will be blessed. In the Kingdom, they will be filled with good food; they will never hunger again.

'Those who mourn will be blessed; those who weep now will be blessed, because when the Kingdom comes, they will be comforted, and they will laugh with joy.

'Those who are scorned and hated will be blessed. Those who are persecuted, and lied about, and defamed, and slandered, and exiled – they will be blessed. Remember the prophets, think of how badly they were treated in their time, and be glad if people treat you the same way; because when the Kingdom comes, you will be rejoicing, believe me.

'The merciful, the kindly, the meek – they will be blessed. They will inherit the earth.

'Those who are pure in heart and think no evil of others – they will be blessed.

'Those who make peace between enemies, those

who solve bitter disputes – they will be blessed. They are the children of God.

'But beware, and remember what I tell you: there are some who will be cursed, who will never inherit the Kingdom of God. D'you want to know who they are? Here goes:

'Those who are rich will be cursed. They've had all the consolation they're going to get.

'Those whose bellies are full now will be cursed. They will suffer the pangs of hunger everlastingly.

'Those who look at poverty and hunger without concern, and turn away with a laugh on their lips, will be cursed; they will have plenty to mourn about; they will weep for ever.

'Those who are well-spoken of, and praised by the powerful, and flattered and fawned over by loud voices in public places, will be cursed. They will have no place in the Kingdom.'

The people cheered at these words, and crowded close to hear more of what Jesus was saying.

Christ is Saved by the Stranger

But at the edge of the crowd someone had noticed what Christ was doing as he noted down the words of Jesus, and said 'A spy! Here's a spy from the Romans – throw him off the mountain!'

Before Christ could defend himself, another voice spoke beside him:

'No, friend, you're wrong. This man is one of us. He's writing down the words of the teacher so he can take them and tell others the good news.'

Christ's accuser was convinced, and turned back to listen to Jesus, forgetting Christ in a moment. Christ saw that the man who had defended him was none other than the stranger, the priest whose name he had not managed to learn.

'Come aside with me for a moment,' said the stranger.

They withdrew from the crowd, and sat under the shade of a tamarisk.

'Am I doing the right thing?' said Christ. 'I

wanted to be sure I heard him correctly, in case there was any judgement later.'

'It is an excellent thing to do,' said the stranger. 'Sometimes there is a danger that people might misinterpret the words of a popular speaker. The statements need to be edited, the meanings clarified, the complexities unravelled for the simple-of-understanding. In fact, I want you to continue. Keep a record of what your brother says, and I shall collect your reports from time to time, so that we can begin the work of interpretation.'

'These words that Jesus is saying,' said Christ, 'they might be seditious, I think. The man thought I was a Roman spy . . . It wouldn't be surprising if the Romans did take an interest, would it?'

'Very shrewdly observed,' said the stranger. 'That's exactly what we have to bear in mind. Political matters are delicate and dangerous, and it requires a subtle mind and a strong nerve to negotiate them safely. I'm sure we can rely on you.'

And with a friendly squeeze of Christ's shoulder, the stranger got to his feet and moved away. There were a dozen questions that Christ wanted to ask him, but before he could utter a

word, the stranger was lost in the crowd. From
the way he had spoken about political affairs,
Christ wondered if his first guess had been right:
perhaps the stranger was not just a priest, but a
member of the Sanhedrin. That was the council
that settled all doctrinal and judicial matters
among the Jews, as well as dealing with Jewish
relations with the Romans, and its members, of
course, were men of great wisdom.

Jesus Continues his Sermon
on the Mountain

Christ took his tablet and stylus and moved to a place where he could hear what his brother was saying. It seemed that someone had asked Jesus to tell them about the law, and whether what it said was still valid in the time of the Kingdom of God.

'Don't anyone think I'm telling you to abandon the law and the prophets,' Jesus said. 'I haven't come here to abolish them. I'm here to fulfil them. I'm telling you truly: not one word, not one letter of the law will be superseded until heaven and earth pass away. If you break one of these laws, even the least of them, beware.'

'But there are degrees, aren't there, master?' someone called out. 'A little sin isn't as bad as a big sin, surely?'

'You know there's a commandment against murder. Where would you draw the line? Would you say murder is wrong, but beating someone is maybe a little less wrong, and just being angry with them isn't wrong at all? I'm telling you that if you're angry with a brother or a sister, by which I mean anyone at all, even if you've just got a grudge against them, don't dare to go and offer a gift in the temple until you've made your peace with them. Do that first of all.

'And I won't have any talk about little sins and big sins. That won't wash in the Kingdom of God. The same goes for adultery. You know the commandment against adultery: it says *don't do it*. It doesn't say "You must not commit adultery, but it's all right to think about it." It isn't. Every time you look at a woman with lustful thoughts, you're already committing adultery with her in your heart. Don't do it. And if your eyes keep looking that way, pluck them out. You think adultery is bad, but divorce is all right? You're wrong: if you divorce your wife for any reason other than her unchastity, you cause her to commit adultery when she marries again. And if you marry a divorced woman, *you* commit adultery. Marriage is a serious business. So is hell. And that's where you'll go if you think that as long as you avoid the big sins, you can get away with the little ones.'

'You said we mustn't be violent, master, but

if someone attacks you, surely you can fight back?'

'"An eye for an eye and a tooth for a tooth"? Is that what you're thinking about? Don't do it. If anyone hits you on the right cheek, offer him the left as well. If anyone wants to take your coat away, give him your cloak to go with it. If he forces you to go one mile, go two. You know why that is? Because you should love your enemy, that's why. Yes, you heard me right: love your enemies, and pray for them. Think of God your Father in heaven, and do as he does. He makes the sun rise on the wicked as well as on the good; he sends the rain to fall on the righteous as well as the unrighteous. What's the good of loving only those who love you? Why, even a tax-collector does that. And if you care only for your brothers and sisters, you're doing no more than the Gentiles. Be perfect.'

Christ wrote this all down diligently, taking care to inscribe 'These are the words that Jesus spoke' on each tablet, so no one should think they were his own opinions.

Someone was asking about almsgiving.

'Good question,' said Jesus. 'What you should

do when you give alms is to shut up about it. Keep silent. You know the sort of people who make a great spectacle of their generosity: don't do as they do. Let no one know when you give, or how much you give, or what cause you give it to. Don't even let your left hand know what your right hand is doing. Your Father in heaven will see, don't worry about that.

'And while I'm talking about keeping quiet, here's another thing to be secret about: and that's prayer. Don't be like those ostentatious hypocrites who pray out loud and let the whole neighbour-hood know about their piety. Go to your room, shut the door, pray in silence and in secret. Your Father will hear. And have you ever heard the Gentiles pray? On and on, yakkety yak, blah blah blah, as if the very sound of their voices were music in the ears of God. Don't be like them. There's no need to tell God what you're asking for; he knows already.

'This is how you should pray. You should say:

'Father in heaven, your name is holy.

'Your Kingdom is coming, and your will shall be done on earth as it's done in heaven.

'Give us today the bread we need.

'And forgive our debts, as we shall forgive those who are indebted to us.

'And don't let the evil one tempt us more than we can resist.

'Because the Kingdom and the power and the glory belong to you for ever.

'So be it.'

'Master,' someone called out, 'if the Kingdom is coming, as you say, how should we live? Should we carry on our trades, should we build houses and raise families and pay taxes as we've always done, or has everything changed now we know about the Kingdom?'

'You're right, friend, everything has changed. There's no need to worry about what you're going to eat or drink, where you're going to sleep, what you're going to wear. Look at the birds: do they sow or reap? Do they gather wheat into the barn? They don't do any of those things, and yet their Father in heaven feeds them every day. Don't you think you're more valuable than the birds? And think what worrying does: has anyone ever added a single hour to the length of his life by worrying about it?

'And think about clothing. Look at the lilies in

the field, how beautiful they are. Not even Solomon in all his splendour looked as glorious as a wild flower. And if God clothes the grass of the field like that, don't you think he'll take even more care of you? You with little faith! I've told you before: don't behave like the Gentiles. They're the ones who fret about things like that. So stop worrying about tomorrow; tomorrow will take care of itself. Today has enough trouble of its own.'

'What should we do when we see someone else doing wrong?' called out one man. 'Should we try and put them straight?'

'Who are you to judge anyone else?' said Jesus. 'You point out the speck in your neighbour's eye, and you don't notice the plank in your own. Take the plank out of your eye first, and then you can see to take the speck out of your neighbour's.

'And you need to see clearly when you look at what you're doing. You need to think and get things right. You don't give meat from sacrifices to the dogs – you might as well give a pearl necklace to a pig. Think what that means.'

'Master, how do we know that all will be well?' said one man.

'You just ask, and it'll be given to you. You

just search, and you'll find. You just knock, and
the door will be opened. You don't believe me?
Consider this: is there a man or woman alive who,
when their child asks for bread, gives them a stone?
Of course not. And if you, sinners every one of
you, know how to give nourishment to a child,
think how much better your Father in heaven will
know how to give good things to those who ask
for them.

'Now I'm going to stop talking soon, but there
are a few more things you need to hear and
remember. There are true prophets, and there are
false prophets, and this is how to tell the difference: look at the fruits they bear. Do you gather
grapes from a thorn bush? Do you look for figs
among the thistles? Of course not, because a bad
tree can't bear good fruit, and a good tree doesn't
bear bad fruit. You will know true prophets and
false prophets by the fruits they bear. And a tree
that bears bad fruit is cut down in the end, and
thrown on the fire.

'And remember this: take the hard road, not
the easy one. The road that leads to life is a hard
one, and it passes through a narrow gate, but the
road to destruction is easy, and the gate is broad.

Plenty take the easy road; few take the hard one. Your job is to find the hard one, and go by that.

'If you hear these words of mine, and act on them, you'll be like a wise man who builds his house on a rock. The rain falls, the floods come, the winds howl and beat on the house, but it doesn't fall, because it's been founded on a rock. But if you hear my words and don't act on them, you'll be like a foolish man who builds his house on sand. And what happens when the rain falls and the floods come and the winds beat against it? The house falls down – and it falls with a great smash.

'And this is the final thing I'll say to you: do to others as you hope they would do to you.

'This is the law and the prophets, this is every-thing you need to know.'

Christ watched as the crowd moved away, and listened to what they said.

'He's not like the scribes,' said one.

'He talks as if he knows things.'

'I never heard straight talking like that before!'

'That's not the sort of waffle you get from the usual preachers. This man knows what he's talking about.'

And Christ considered everything he'd heard that day, and pondered it deeply as he transcribed the words from his tablet on to a scroll; but he said nothing to anyone.

The Death of John

All this time John the Baptist had been captive in prison. King Herod Antipas really wanted to put him to death, but he knew that John was popular with the people, and he feared what they might do in response. Now the king's wife – the one John had criticised him for marrying – was called Herodias, and she had a daughter called Salome. When the court was celebrating the king's birthday Salome danced for him, and pleased everyone so much that Herod promised to give her whatever she asked for. Her mother prompted her, and she said 'I want the head of John the Baptist on a platter.'

Herod was privately dismayed. But he had promised in front of his guests, and he couldn't back down; so he ordered the executioner to go to the prison and behead John at once. It was done, and the head was brought, just as Salome had demanded, on a platter. The girl gave it to Herodias. As for the Baptist's body, his followers came to the prison and took it away to be buried.

Feeding the Crowd

Knowing how highly Jesus had regarded John, some of those followers of the Baptist came to Galilee and told him what had happened; and Jesus, wanting to be alone, went out in a boat by himself. No one knew where he had gone, but Christ let one or two people know, and soon the word got around. When Jesus came ashore in what he thought would be a lonely place, he found a great crowd waiting for him.

He felt sorry for them, and began to speak, and some people who were sick felt themselves uplifted by his presence, and declared themselves cured.

It was nearly evening, and Jesus's disciples said to him 'This is the middle of nowhere, and all these people need to eat. Tell them to go away now, and find a village where they can buy food. They can't stay here all night.'

Jesus said 'They don't need to go away. As for food, what have you got between you?'

'Five loaves and two fishes, master; nothing else.'

'Give them to me,' said Jesus.

He took the loaves and the fishes, and blessed them, and then said to the crowd 'See how I share this food out? You do the same. There'll be enough for everyone.'

And sure enough, it turned out that one man had brought some barley cakes, and another had a couple of apples, and a third had some dried fish, and a fourth had a pocketful of raisins, and so on; and between them all, there was plenty to go round. No one was left hungry.

And Christ, watching it all and taking notes, recorded this as another miracle.

The Informant, and the
Canaanite Woman

But Christ couldn't follow Jesus everywhere. It would have attracted notice, and by this time he was sure he should remain very much in the background. Accordingly, he asked one of the disciples to tell him what happened when he wasn't there – keeping it quiet, of course.

'There's no need to tell Jesus about it,' Christ told him. 'But I'm keeping a record of his wise words and his marvellous deeds, and it would be a great help if I could rely on an accurate report.'

'Who is this for?' said the disciple. 'It's not for the Romans, is it? Or the Pharisees or the Sadducees?'

'No, no. It's for the sake of the Kingdom of God. Every kingdom has its historian, or how would we know of the great deeds of David and Solomon? That's my role: just a simple historian. Will you help me?'

The disciple agreed, and soon he had something

to tell. It happened when Jesus was away from Galilee, travelling in the coastal region between Tyre and Sidon. Evidently his fame had already reached those parts, because a woman from that district, a Canaanite, heard he was passing by and came running to cry out:

'Have mercy on me, son of David!'

She addressed him like that despite the fact that she was a Gentile. However, it made little impression on Jesus, who took no notice of her, though the woman's cries began to annoy the disciples who were with him.

'Send her away, master!' they said.

Finally he turned to her and said 'I haven't come to speak to the Gentiles. I'm here for the house of Israel, not for you.'

'But please, master!' she said. 'My daughter is tormented by a demon, and I've got no one else to ask!' And she threw herself to her knees in front of him and said 'Lord, help me!'

'Should I take food meant for the children, and throw it to the dogs?' Jesus said.

But this woman was clever enough to find an answer, and she said 'Even the dogs can eat the crumbs that fall from the master's table.'

That answer pleased him, and he said 'Woman, your faith has saved your daughter. Go home and find her well.'

The disciple reported this, and Christ wrote it down.

The Woman with the Ointment

Shortly afterwards Jesus had another encounter with a woman, and the disciple reported this as well. It happened in Magdala at a private dinner in the house of a Pharisee called Simon. A woman of the city heard he was there, and came bringing Jesus a gift of ointment in an alabaster jar. The host let her in and she knelt before Jesus and wept, bathing his feet with her tears, drying them with her hair, and anointing them with the precious unguent.

The host said quietly to the disciple who was Christ's informant 'If this master of yours were really a prophet, he'd know what kind of woman this is – she's a notorious sinner.'

But Jesus overheard, and said 'Simon, come here. I want to ask you a question.'

'Certainly,' said the Pharisee.

'Suppose there's a man who's owed money by two others. One owes him five hundred denarii, and the other owes him fifty. Now, suppose they can't pay, and he forgives them and wipes off their debts. Which of them will be more grateful?'

'I suppose the one who owed five hundred,' said Simon.

'Exactly,' said Jesus. 'Now, you see this woman? You see what she's doing? When I came into your house you offered me no water to wash my feet, but here she is bathing them with her tears. You didn't greet me with a kiss, but from the moment she's come in she hasn't stopped kissing my feet. You gave me no oil, but she's lavished this precious ointment on me. There's a reason for that: she has committed great sins, but they've been forgiven, and that's why she loves so deeply. You haven't committed many sins, so it means little to you to know that they've been forgiven. And you love me so much the less as a result.'

The others at the dinner were astonished at his words, but the disciple took care to remember them, and reported them faithfully to Christ, who wrote everything down. As for the woman, she became a follower of Jesus, and one of the most faithful.

The Stranger Talks of
Truth and History

Christ never knew when the stranger would come
to him. The next time he appeared it was late at
night, and the stranger's voice spoke quietly
through his window:

'Christ, come and tell me what has been
happening.'

Christ gathered his scrolls together and left the
house on tiptoe. The stranger beckoned him away
from the town and up on to the dark hillside where
they could talk without being overheard.

The stranger listened without interrupting
while Christ told him everything Jesus had done
since the sermon on the mountain.

'Well done,' said the stranger. 'This is excellent
work. How did you hear about the events in Tyre
and Sidon? You did not go there, I think.'

'I asked one of his disciples to keep me
informed,' said Christ. 'Without letting Jesus
know, of course. I hope that was permitted?'

'You have a real talent for this task.'

'Thank you, sir. There is one thing that would help me do it better, though. If I knew the reason for your enquiries I could look more purposefully. Are you from the Sanhedrin?'

'Is that what you think? And what do you understand of the function of the Sanhedrin?'

'Why, it's the body that determines great matters of law and doctrine. And of course it deals with taxes and administrative business, and – and so on. Naturally I don't mean to imply that it's a mere bureaucracy, although such things are, of course, necessary in human affairs . . . '

'What did you tell the disciple who is your informant?'

'I told him that I was writing the history of the Kingdom of God, and that he would be helping in that great task.'

'A very good answer. You could do worse than apply it to your own question. In helping me, you are helping to write that history. But there is more, and this is not for everyone to know: in writing about what has gone past, we help to shape what will come. There are dark days approaching, turbulent times; if the way to the Kingdom of

God is to be opened, we who know must be prepared to make history the handmaid of posterity and not its governor. *What should have been* is a better servant of the Kingdom than *what was*. I am sure you understand me.'

'I do,' said Christ. 'And, sir, if you read my scrolls—'

'I shall read them with close attention, and with gratitude for your unselfish and courageous work.'

The stranger took the bundle of scrolls under his cloak, and stood up to leave.

'Remember what I told you when we first met,' he said. 'There is time, and there is what is beyond time. History belongs to time, but truth belongs to what is beyond time. In writing of things as they should have been, you are letting truth into history. You are the word of God.'

'When will you come again?' said Christ.

'I shall come when I am needed. And when I come again, we shall talk about your brother.'

A moment later, the stranger had disappeared in the darkness of the hillside. Christ sat for a long time in the cold wind, pondering on what the stranger had said. The words 'we who know' were some of the most thrilling he had ever heard. And he began to wonder if he had been right to think that the stranger came from the Sanhedrin; the man hadn't exactly denied it, but he seemed to have a range of knowledge and a point of view that was quite unlike those of any lawyer or rabbi Christ had ever heard.

In fact, now that he thought about it, Christ realised that the stranger was unlike anyone he had ever come across. What he said was so strikingly different from anything Christ had read in the Torah, or heard in the synagogue, that he began to wonder whether the stranger was a Jew at all. He spoke Aramaic perfectly, but it was much more likely, given all the circumstances, that he was a Gentile, perhaps a Greek philosopher from Athens or Alexandria.

And Christ went home to his bed, full of humble joy at his own prescience; for hadn't he spoken to Jesus in the wilderness about the need to include the Gentiles in the great organisation that would embody the Kingdom of God?

'Who Do You Say I Am?'

Around that time, King Herod began to hear rumours of this man who was going about the country healing the sick and speaking words of prophecy. He was alarmed, because some people were saying that John the Baptist had been raised from the dead. Herod knew full well that John was dead, for hadn't he himself ordered the man's execution, and offered his head on a platter to Salome? But then other rumours began to circulate: this new preacher was Elijah himself, returned to Israel after hundreds of years; or he was this prophet or that one, come back to chastise the Jews and foretell catastrophe.

Naturally, all this concerned Herod deeply, and he sent out word that he would be glad to see the preacher in person. He was unsuccessful in this attempt to meet Jesus, but Christ noted it down as evidence of how well known his brother was becoming.

To go by what his informant told him, though,

it was clear to Christ that Jesus was not happy about this increasing fame. On one occasion, in the region of the Decapolis, he cured a deaf man who had a speech impediment, and ordered the man's friends to say nothing about it, but they went and told everyone they knew. Another time, in Bethsaida, he restored the sight of a blind man, and when the man could see again Jesus told him to go straight home and not even go into the village; but word got out about that too. Then there was an occasion in Caesarea Philippi when Jesus was walking along with his disciples, and they were talking about the public following he was gathering.

'Who do people say I am?' Jesus asked.

'Some say Elijah,' said one disciple.

Another said 'They think you're John the Baptist, come back to life.'

'They say all kinds of names – prophets, mainly,' said a third. 'Like Jeremiah, for instance.'

'But who do you say I am?' said Jesus.

And Peter said 'You're the Messiah.'

'Is that what you think?' said Jesus. 'Well, you'd better hold your tongue about it. I don't want to hear that sort of talk, you understand?'

When Christ heard about this he hardly knew how to record it for the Greek stranger. He was confused, and wrote it down in the disciple's words, and then erased them and tried to formulate the expression to be more in keeping with what the stranger had said about truth and history; but that confused him further, so that all his wits seemed to lie scattered about him instead of working firmly at his command.

Finally he gathered himself and wrote down what the disciple had told him, up to the point where Peter spoke. Then a thought came to him, and he wrote something new. Knowing how highly Jesus regarded Peter, he wrote that Jesus had praised him for seeing something that only his Father in heaven could have revealed, and that he had gone on to make a pun on Peter's name, saying that he was the rock on which Jesus would build his church. That church would be so firmly established that the gates of hell would not prevail against it. Finally, Christ wrote that Jesus had promised to give Peter the keys of heaven.

When he had written these words, he trembled. He wondered if he were being presumptuous in making Jesus express the thoughts that he himself had put to his brother in the wilderness, about the need for an organisation that would embody the Kingdom on earth. Jesus had scorned the idea. But then Christ remembered what the stranger had said: that in writing like this, he was letting truth from beyond time into history, and thus making history the handmaid of posterity and not its governor; and he felt uplifted.

Pharisees and Sadducees

Jesus continued his mission, speaking and preaching and offering parables to illustrate his teaching, and Christ wrote down much of what he said, letting the truth beyond time guide his stylus whenever he could. There were some sayings, though, that he could neither leave out nor alter, because they caused such a stir among the disciples and among the crowds that came to listen wherever Jesus went. Everyone knew what he had said, and many people talked about his words; it would be noticed if they were not in the record.

Many of these sayings concerned children and the family, and some of them cut Christ to the quick. Once, on the road to Capernaum, the disciples were arguing. Jesus had heard their raised voices, but was walking apart from them and didn't hear what they were saying.

When they went into the house where they were to stay he said:

'What were you arguing about on the way?'

They fell silent, because they were embarrassed. Finally one of them said:

'We were discussing which of us was the most important, master.'

'Were you, indeed. Come around here, all of you.'

They stood in front of him. Now in that house there was a little child, and Jesus picked him up and showed him to the disciples.

'Whoever wants to be first,' he said, 'must be last of all and servant of all. Unless you change and become like little children, you will never enter the Kingdom of heaven. Whoever becomes as humble as this child will be the most important in heaven. And whoever welcomes a child like this in my name welcomes me.'

Another time, Jesus had stopped to sit down, and people brought their little children to him to be blessed.

'Not now!' the disciples said. 'Go away! The master is resting.'

Jesus heard them, and was angry.

'Don't speak to these good people like that,' he said. 'Let them bring their children here. Who else do you think the Kingdom of God is for? It belongs to them.'

The disciples stood aside, and the people carried their children to Jesus, who blessed them, and took them in his arms, and kissed them.

Speaking to his disciples as well as to the parents of the children, he said 'You should all be like little children when it comes to the Kingdom, otherwise you will never enter it. So be careful. Whoever makes it difficult for one of these little ones to come to me, it would be better for them if a millstone were hung about their neck and they were drowned in the depths of the sea.'

Christ noted down the words, admiring the vigour of the imagery while regretting the thinking behind it; because if it were true that only children could be admitted to the Kingdom, what was the value of such adult qualities as responsibility, forethought, and wisdom? Surely the Kingdom would need those as well.

On another occasion, some Pharisees tried to test Jesus by asking about divorce. Jesus had spoken about that subject in his sermon on the mountain, but they had spotted what they thought was a contradiction in what he had said.

'Is divorce lawful?' they said.

'Haven't you read the scriptures?' was Jesus's reply. 'Don't you remember how the Lord God made Adam and Eve male and female, and declared that a man should leave his father and his mother and join his wife, and the two of them shall become one flesh? Had you forgotten that? So no one should separate what God has joined together.'

'Ah,' they said, 'then why did Moses make his specification about a certificate of divorce? He would not have done that if God had forbidden it.'

'God tolerates it now, but did he institute it in Eden? Was there any need for divorce then? No. Man and woman then were created to live perfectly together. It was only after the coming of sin that divorce became necessary. And when the Kingdom comes, as it will, and men and women live together perfectly once more, there will be no need for divorce.'

The Sadducees also tried to trick Jesus with a problem concerning marriage. Now the Sadducees didn't believe in resurrection or an afterlife, and they thought they could get the better of Jesus by asking him a question about that.

'If a man dies without having children,' they

said, 'it's the custom for his brother to marry the widow, and beget children for him. Is that not so?'

'That is the custom,' said Jesus.

'Well, now: suppose there are seven brothers. The first marries, and dies childless, so the widow marries the second brother. The same thing happens again: the husband dies childless, and she marries the next, all the way down to the seventh brother. Then the woman herself dies. So – when the dead are resurrected, whose wife will she be? Because she's married all of them.'

'You're wrong,' said Jesus. 'You don't know the scriptures, and you don't know the power of God. When the dead are resurrected they will neither marry nor be given in marriage. They'll live like the angels. As for the resurrection of the dead, you forget what God said to Moses when he spoke from the burning bush. He said "I am the God of Abraham, the God of Isaac, and the God of Jacob." Would he have spoken in the present tense if they were not alive? He is not the God of the dead; he is the God of the living.'

The Sadducees had to retreat, confounded.

Jesus and the Family

But for all Jesus's defence of marriage, and of children, he had little to say in favour of the family, or of comfortable prosperity. On one occasion he said to a crowd of people who wanted to follow him 'If you don't hate your father and your mother, your brothers and sisters, your wife, your children, you'll never become my disciple.' And Christ remembered Jesus's words when he'd been told that his mother and brothers and sisters had come to see him: he had rejected them, and claimed that he had no family except those who did the will of God. To hear his brother speak of hating one's family worried Christ; he would not have chosen to write those words, but too many people had heard Jesus say them.

Then one day in Christ's hearing Jesus told a story that disturbed him more greatly still.

'There was a man who had two sons, one quiet and good, the other wild and unruly. The wild one said to his father "Father, you're going to divide the property between us anyway; let me have my share now." The father did, and the wild son went away to another country, and squandered all his money in drink and gambling and debauchery, until he had nothing left.

'Then there came a famine in the country where he was living, and the wild son found himself in such desperate need that he hired himself out as a swineherd. He was so hungry that he would have been glad to be able to eat the husks that the pigs were eating. In his despair he thought of his home, and said to himself "At home there are my father's hired hands, and every one of them has all the bread he wants, and to spare; and here I am, dying of hunger. I'll go home and confess to my father and beg his forgiveness, and ask him to take me on as a hired hand."

'So he set off towards home, and when his father heard he was coming he was filled with compassion, and he hurried out of the town to meet him, and embraced him and kissed him. The son said "Father, I've sinned against heaven and I've sinned against you; I don't deserve to be called your son. Just let me work for you like one of the hired hands."

'But the father said to the servants "Bring out the best robe, and some sandals for my son's feet, and hurry! And prepare a feast – the best of every-thing – because this dear son of mine was dead, and here he is alive again; he was lost, and now he's found!"

'But the other son, the quiet one, the good one, heard the sounds of celebration and saw what was going on, and said to his father:

'"Father, why are you preparing a feast for him? I have been at home all the time, I have never dis-obeyed your commands, and yet you've never prepared a feast for me. My brother walked away without thinking of the rest of us, he squandered all his money, he has no thought for his family or anyone else."

'And the father said "Son, you're at home all the time. All that I have is yours. But when someone comes home after being away, it's right and proper to prepare a feast in celebration. And your brother was dead, and he's come to life again; he was lost, and he's been found."'

When Christ heard that story, he felt as if he had been stripped naked in front of the whole crowd. He had no idea that his brother had seen him there, but he must have done, in order to mortify him so exquisitely. All Christ could hope was that no one had noticed, and he resolved to keep even more discreetly to the background in future.

Difficult Stories

Not long afterwards, Jesus told another story that seemed to Christ unfair. Nor was he the only listener to react like that: many people could not understand it at all, and discussed it with one another afterwards. Someone had asked Jesus what the Kingdom of heaven would be like, and he said:

'It's like a farmer who went out early in the morning to hire labourers for his vineyard. He struck a deal with them for the usual daily wage, and they set to work. A couple of hours later he was passing through the market place and he saw some other workers standing idle, and he said "You want a job? Go to my vineyard and I'll pay you whatever's fair." Off they went, and he went on his way, and then came past again at noon, and then once more halfway through the afternoon, and each time saw some other men standing about, and said the same to them.

'Finally, about five o'clock, he came through

the market one more time, saw another group there, and said "Why are you standing idle all day long?"

'"No one has hired us," they said. So he hired them on the same terms.

'When it was evening, he said to his manager "Call the men to come and get their pay, starting with the last, and then going back to the first."

'When the five o'clock workers came, he gave them each a full day's wage, as he did to all the others. The workers who had been hired in the early morning grumbled about this, and said "You're giving these men, who've only worked for one hour, the same as us, who've been labouring all day in the scorching heat?"

'The farmer said "My friend, you agreed to accept a day's wages for a day's work, and that's exactly what you've got. Take what you've earned, and go. Aren't I entitled to do whatever I choose with what belongs to me? Because I choose to be good-natured, should that make you ill-natured?"'

Another story that Jesus told was even harder for his listeners to understand, but Christ wrote it down for the stranger in the hope that he could explain it.

'There was a rich farmer who had a manager to look after his business, and complaints began to come to him about the way this man was dealing with his affairs. So he called the manager to come and see him, and said "I've been hearing things about you that I don't like. I'm going to dismiss you, but first I want a full account of everything that's owed to me."

'And the manager thought "What in the world am I going to do now? I'm not strong enough for manual labour, and I'm ashamed to beg . . . " So he came up with a plan to ensure that other people would look after him when he was out of work.

'He called his employer's debtors to him one by one. He asked the first one "How much do you owe my employer?" and the man said "A hundred jars of oil." "Sit down quickly," said the manager, "take your account, and write fifty instead."

'To the next one he said "How much do you owe?" "A hundred bushels of wheat." "Here's your account. Cross out a hundred, and make it eighty."

'And he did the same with the rest of the

debtors. Now, what did the master say when he heard about this? Whatever you think, you're wrong. What he did was to commend the dishonest manager for his shrewdness.'

What Jesus seemed to be saying with these stories, Christ thought, was something horrible: that God's love was arbitrary and undeserved, almost like a lottery. Jesus's friendship with tax-collectors and prostitutes and other undesirable characters must also have been part of this radical attitude; he seemed to have a real scorn for what was commonly thought of as virtue. He once told a story about two men, a Pharisee and a tax-collector, who both went to the temple to pray. The Pharisee stood by himself looking up to heaven and said 'God, I thank you that I'm not like other men, a thief, an adulterer, a swindler, or like that tax-collector over there. I fast twice a week, and I give away a tenth of my income.' But the tax-collector didn't dare to look up; he kept his eyes down and beat his breast, saying 'God, I beg you, be merciful to me, a sinner.' And this, and not the other, Jesus told his listeners, was the man who would enter the Kingdom.

It was a popular message, no doubt; the

common people delighted to hear about men and women such as themselves winning undeserved success. But it troubled Christ, and he longed to ask the stranger about it.

The Stranger Transfigured;
A Coming Crisis

He soon had his chance. As he walked one evening beside the Sea of Galilee, thinking he was alone, he found the stranger beside him.

He was startled, and said 'Sir! I didn't see you. Forgive me for not greeting you – had you been beside me for some time? My thoughts were elsewhere.'

'I am always close to you,' said the stranger, and they fell into step and walked along together.

'When we spoke last,' said Christ, 'you said that next time we would talk about my brother.'

'And so we shall. What is his future, do you think?'

'His future – I can't tell, sir. He's stirring up a good deal of animosity. I worry that if he's not careful he might meet the same fate as John, the Baptist, or else provoke the Romans as the Zealots are doing.'

'But is he careful?'

'No. I'd say he was reckless. But to him, you see, the Kingdom of God is coming very soon, and it makes no sense to be cautious and prudent.'

'To *him*, you say? You mean you don't think he's right? This is just a guess of his, and he might be mistaken?'

'Not quite that,' said Christ. 'I think we have a difference of emphasis. I believe the Kingdom is coming, of course I do. But he thinks it will come without warning, because God is impulsive and arbitrary. That's at the root of it.'

He told the stranger the parables that had troubled him.

'I see,' said the stranger. 'And you? What do you think of God?'

'I think he is just. Virtue must play some part in whether we are rewarded or punished, or else why be virtuous? What the law and the prophets say – what Jesus himself says – doesn't make sense otherwise. It's just not consistent.'

'I can see how it must trouble you.'

They walked on a little way in silence.

'And besides,' said Christ, 'there is the matter of the Gentiles.'

He left it there, to see how his companion

would respond. If, as he thought, the man was Greek, he would naturally be interested.

But the stranger merely said 'Go on.'

'Well,' said Christ, 'Jesus preaches only to the Jews. He's said clearly that Gentiles are dogs, for example. It was on the scrolls I gave you last time.'

'I remember. But you don't agree?'

Christ was aware that if this man had come to tempt him into rash words, this was exactly the way he would do it: lead him by soft questions.

'Again, sir,' he said carefully, 'I think it's a matter of emphasis. I know that the Jews are the beloved people of God – the scripture says that. And yet God surely created the Gentiles too, and there are good men and women among them. Whatever form the Kingdom may take, it will surely be a new dispensation, and it would not be surprising, given the infinite mercy and justice of God, to find his love extending to the Gentiles . . . But these mysteries are deep, and I may be wrong. I wish, sir, you would tell me what the truth is. It lies beyond time, as you told me, but my knowledge is lacking, and my vision clouded.'

'Come with me,' said the stranger.

And he led Christ up the hillside to a place

where the setting sun illuminated everything brightly. The stranger was wearing clothes of pure white, and the glare from them was dazzling.

'I asked about your brother,' said the stranger, 'because it's clear that a crisis in the world is coming, and because of it you and he both will be remembered in times to come just as Moses and Elijah are remembered now. We must make sure, you and I, that the accounts of these days give due weight to the miraculous nature of the events the world is passing through. For example, the voice from the cloud you heard at his baptism.'

'I remember my mother told you about that . . . But did you know that when I told Jesus about it I said that the voice spoke of him?'

'That is exactly why you are the perfect chronicler of these events, my dear Christ, and why your name will shine in equal splendour with his. You know how to present a story so its true meaning shines out with brilliance and clarity. And when you come to assemble the history of what the world is living through now, you will add to the outward and visible events their inward and spiritual significance; so, for example, when you look down on the story as God looks down on time, you will be able to have Jesus foretell to his disciples, as it were in truth, the events to come of which, in history, he was unaware.'

'Since you spoke to me of the difference between them, I have always tried to let the truth irradiate the history.'

'And he is the history, and you are the truth,' said the stranger. 'But just as truth knows more than history, so you will have to be wiser than he is. You will have to step outside time, and see the necessity for things that those within time find distressing or repugnant. You will have to see, my dear Christ, with the vision of God and the angels. You will see the shadows and the darkness without which the light would have no brilliance. You will need courage and resolution; you will need all your strength. Are you ready for that vision?'

'Yes, sir, I am.'

'Then we shall speak again soon. Close your eyes and sleep now.'

And Christ felt overpowering tiredness, and lay down where he was on the ground. When he awoke it was dark, and he felt he had experienced a dream stranger than any other he had known. But the dream had solved one mystery, because he knew now that the stranger was no ordinary teacher, no member of the Sanhedrin, no Greek philosopher: he was not a human being at all. He could only be an angel.

And he kept the vision of the angel, his white garments dazzling with light, and resolved to let the truth of that vision into the history of his brother.

Jesus Debates with a Lawyer;
The Good Samaritan

For most of the time Christ kept out of the way of Jesus, because he could rely on the words of his informant. He knew his spy was trustworthy, because occasionally he checked the man's report by asking others what Jesus had said here, or done there, and found always that his informant was strictly accurate.

But when Christ heard that Jesus was going to preach in this town or that, he sometimes attended to hear for himself, always remaining inconspicuous at the back of the assembly. On one occasion when he did this, he heard Jesus questioned by a lawyer. Men of the law often tried their skill against Jesus, but Jesus was able to deal with most of them, though he frequently did so by what Christ thought were unfair means. Telling a story, as he so often did, introduced extra-legal elements into the discourse: persuading people by manipulating their emotions was all very well to gain a debating point, but it left the question of law unanswered.

This time the lawyer said to him 'Teacher, what must I do to inherit eternal life?'

Christ listened closely as Jesus responded:

'You're a lawyer, are you? Well, tell me what the law says.'

'You must love the Lord God with all your heart, and with all your soul, and with all your strength, and with all your mind. And you must love your neighbour as you love yourself.'

'That's it,' said Jesus, 'you've got it. You know the law. Do that, and you'll live.'

But the man was a lawyer, after all, and he wanted to show that he had a question for every-thing. So he said 'Ah, but tell me this: who is my neighbour?'

So Jesus told this story:

'Once there was a man, a Jew like yourself, going along the road from Jerusalem to Jericho. And in the middle of his journey he was set on by a band of robbers, who stripped him, beat him, stole everything he had, and left him there by the roadside half-dead.

'Well, dangerous as it is, it's a busy road, and

soon afterwards, along came a priest. He took one look at the man covered in blood at the roadside, and decided to look the other way and go on without stopping. Then along came a temple official, and he too decided not to get involved; he passed by as quickly as he could.

'But the next to come along was a Samaritan. He saw the wounded man, and he stopped to help. He poured wine on his wounds to disinfect them, and oil to soothe them, and he helped the man up on to his own donkey and took him to an inn. He gave the innkeeper money to look after him, and said "If you need to spend more than this, keep an account, and I'll pay it next time I'm passing."

'So here's a question for you, in answer to your question of me: which of these three men, the priest, the official, and the Samaritan, was a neighbour to the man who was robbed on the Jericho road?'

The lawyer could only answer 'The one who helped him.'

'That's all you need to know,' said Jesus. 'Off you go, and do the same thing.'

Christ knew as he wrote it down that, for

all its unfairness, people would remember that story much longer than they'd remember a legal definition.

Mary and Martha

One day Jesus and some of his followers were invited to eat with two sisters, one called Mary and the other called Martha. Christ's informant told him what happened that evening. Jesus had been speaking, and Mary was sitting among the people listening to him, while Martha was busy preparing the meal.

At one point Martha came in to rebuke Mary: 'You let the bread burn! Look! I ask you to be careful with it, and you just forget all about it! How can I do three or four things at once?'

Mary said 'The bread is not as important as this. I'm listening to the master's words. He's only here for one night. We can eat bread any time.'

'Master, what do you think?' said Martha. 'Shouldn't she help me, if I've asked her to? There are a lot of us here tonight. I can't do it all on my own.'

Jesus said 'Mary, you can hear my words again, because there are others here to remember them.

But once you've burnt the bread, no one can eat it. Go and help your sister.'

When Christ heard about this, he knew it would be another of those sayings of Jesus that would be better as truth than as history.

Christ and the Prostitute

On the few occasions when Christ came close to Jesus, he did his best to avoid contact with him, but from time to time someone would ask him who he was, what he was doing, whether he was one of Jesus's followers, and so on. He managed to deal with questions of this kind quite easily by adopting a manner of mild courtesy and friendliness, and by making himself inconspicuous. In truth, he attracted little attention and kept to himself, but like any other man he sometimes longed for company.

Once, in a town Jesus had not visited before and where his followers were little known, Christ got into conversation with a woman. She was one of the prostitutes Jesus made welcome, but she had not gone in to dinner with the rest of them. When she saw Christ on his own, she said 'Would you like to come to my house?'

Knowing what sort of woman she was, and realising that no one would see them, he agreed.

He followed her to her house, and went in after her, and waited while she looked in the inner room to see that her children were asleep.

When she lit the lamp and looked at him she was startled, and said 'Master, forgive me! The street was dark, and I couldn't see your face.'

'I'm not Jesus,' said Christ. 'I'm his brother.'

'You look so like him. Have you come to me for business?'

He could say nothing, but she understood, and invited him to lie on the bed with her. The business was concluded rapidly, and afterwards Christ felt moved to explain why he had accepted her invitation.

'My brother maintains that sinners will be forgiven more readily than those who are righteous,' he said. 'I have not sinned very much; perhaps I have not sinned enough to earn the forgiveness of God.'

'You came to me not because I tempted you, then, but out of piety? I wouldn't earn much if that was the case with every man.'

'Of course I was tempted. Otherwise I would not have been able to lie with you.'

'Will you tell your brother about this?'

'I don't talk much to my brother. He has never listened to me.'

'You sound bitter.'

'I don't feel bitter. I love my brother. He has a great task, and I wish I could serve him better than I do. If I sound downcast, it's perhaps because I'm conscious of the depth of my failure to be like him.'

'Do you want to be like him?'

'More than anything. He does things out of passion, and I do them out of calculation. I can see further than he can; I can see the consequences of things he doesn't think twice about. But he acts with the whole of himself at every moment, and I'm always holding something back out of caution, or prudence, or because I want to watch and record rather than participate.'

'If you let go of your caution, you might be carried away by passion as he is.'

'No,' said Christ. 'There are some who live by every rule and cling tightly to their rectitude because they fear being swept away by a tempest of passion, and there are others who cling to the rules because they fear that there is no passion there at all, and that if they let go they would simply remain where they are, foolish and unmoved; and they could bear that least of all. Living a life of iron control lets them pretend to themselves that only by the mightiest effort of will can they hold great passions at bay. I am one of those. I know it, and I can do nothing about it.'

'It's something to know it, at least.'

'If my brother wanted to talk about it, he would make it into a story that was unforgettable. All I can do is describe it.'

'And describing it is something, at least.'

'Yes, it is something, but not much.'

'Do you envy your brother, then?'

'I admire him, I love him, I long for his approval. But he cares little for his family; he's often said so. If I vanished he wouldn't notice, if I died he wouldn't care. I think of him all the time, and he thinks of me not at all. I love him, and my love torments me. There are times when I feel like a ghost beside him; as if he alone is real, and I'm just a daydream. But envy him? Do I begrudge him the love and the admiration that so many give him so freely? No. I truly believe that he deserves it all, and more. I want to serve him . . . No, I believe that I am serving him, in ways he will never know about.'

'Was it like that when you were young?'

'He would get into trouble, and I would get him out of it, or plead for him, or distract the grown-ups' attention by a clever trick or a winning remark. He was never grateful; he took it for granted that I would rescue him. And I didn't mind. I was happy to serve him. I am happy to serve him.'

'If you were more like him, you could not serve him so well.'

'I could serve others better.'

Then the woman said 'Sir, am I a sinner?'

'Yes. But my brother would say your sins are forgiven.'

'Do you say that?'

'I believe it to be true.'

'Then, sir, would you do something for me?'

And the woman opened her robe and showed him her breast. It was ravaged with an ulcerating cancer.

'If you believe my sins are forgiven,' she said, 'please heal me.'

Christ turned his head away, and then looked back at her and said 'Your sins are forgiven.'

'Must I believe that too?'

'Yes. I must believe it, and you must believe it.'

'Tell me again.'

'Your sins are forgiven. Truly.'

'How will I know?'

'You must have faith.'

'If I have faith, will I be healed?'

'Yes.'

'I will have faith, if you do, sir.'

'I do.'

'Tell me once more.'

'I have said it . . . Very well: your sins are forgiven.'

'And yet I'm not healed,' she said.

She closed her robe.

Christ said 'And I am not my brother. Didn't I tell you that? Why did you ask me to heal you, if you knew I was not Jesus? Did I ever claim to be able to heal you? I said to you "Your sins are forgiven." If you don't have sufficient faith after you've heard that, the fault is yours.'

The woman turned away and faced the wall, and drew her robe over her head.

Christ left her house. He was ashamed, and he went out of the town and climbed to a quiet place among the rocks, and prayed that his own sins might be forgiven. He wept a little. He was afraid the angel might come to him, and he hid all night.

The Wise and Foolish Girls

Now the time of the Passover was getting close, and this prompted the people who listened to Jesus to ask about the Kingdom again: when will it come? How will we know it? What should we do to be ready for it?

'It'll be like this,' he told them. 'There was a wedding, and ten girls took their lamps and went to meet the bridegroom and welcome him to the banquet. Now five of them took their lamps and nothing else, no spare oil, but the other five were a bit cleverer than that, and they brought some flasks of oil with them.

'Well, the bridegroom was delayed, and time went past, and all of the girls began to feel drowsy and closed their eyes.

'Then at midnight there was a cry: "He's coming! The bridegroom is here!"

'The girls woke up at once and started trimming their lamps. You can see what happened next: the foolish ones discovered that their oil had run out.

'"Give us some of your oil!" they said to the others. "Look, our lamps are going out!"

'And two of the far-seeing ones shared their oil with two of the foolish ones, and all four were admitted to the banquet. Two of the clever ones refused, and the bridegroom shut them out, together with two more foolish ones.

'But the last wise girl said "Lord, we have come to celebrate your wedding, even the least of us. If you won't let us all in, I would rather stay outside with my sisters, even when the last of my oil is gone."

'And for her sake the bridegroom opened the doors of the banquet and admitted them all. Now, where was the Kingdom of heaven? Inside the bridegroom's house? Is that what you think? No, it was outside in the dark with the wise girl and her sisters, even when the last of her oil was gone.'

Christ wrote down every word, but he resolved to improve the story later.

The Stranger Talks of
Abraham and Isaac

Next time the angel came, Christ was in Jericho. He was following Jesus and his disciples as they made their way to Jerusalem for the Passover. Jesus was staying in the house of one of his followers, but Christ had taken a room in a tavern not far away. At midnight he went outside to use the privy. When he turned to go back inside he felt a hand on his shoulder, and knew at once that it was the stranger.

'Events are moving quickly now,' the stranger said. 'We must talk about something important. Take me to your room.'

Once inside, Christ lit the lamp and gathered up the scrolls he had filled.

'Sir, what do you do with these scrolls?' he said.

'I take them to a place of great safety.'

'Will I be able to see them again? I may need to edit and correct the entries, in the light of what I have since learned about truth and history.'

'There will be an opportunity for that, never fear. Now tell me about your brother. What is his mood as he gets closer to Jerusalem?'

'He seems serene and confident, sir. I wouldn't say that has changed at all.'

'Does he speak of what he expects to happen there?'

'Only that the Kingdom will come very soon. Perhaps it will come when he is in the temple.'

'And the disciples? How is your informant? Is he still close to Jesus?'

'I would say he is in the very best position. He is not the closest or the most favoured – Peter and James and John are the men Jesus speaks to most confidentially – but my informant is securely among the middle-ranking followers. His reports are full and trustworthy. I have checked them.'

'We must think about rewarding him at some stage. But now I want to talk to you about something difficult.'

'I am ready, sir.'

'You and I know that for the Kingdom to

flourish, it needs a body of men, and women too, both Jews and Gentiles, faithful followers under the guidance of men of authority and wisdom. And this church – we can call it a church – will need men of formidable organisational powers and deep intellectual penetration, both to conceive and develop the structure of the body and to formulate the doctrines that will hold it together. There are such men, and they are ready and waiting. The church will not lack organisation and doctrine.

'But you will remember, my dear Christ, the story of Abraham and Isaac. God sets his people severe tests. How many men of today would be ready to act like Abraham, prepared to sacrifice his son because the Lord had told him to? How many would be like Isaac, ready to do as his father told him and hold out his hands to be bound, and lie down on the altar, and wait peaceably for the knife in the serene confidence of righteousness?'

'I would,' said Christ at once. 'If that is what God wants, I would do that. If it would serve the Kingdom, yes, I would. If it would serve my brother, yes, yes, I would.'

He spoke eagerly, because he knew that this

would give him the chance to atone for his failure to heal the woman with the cancer. It was his faith that had been insufficient, not hers; he had spoken harshly to her, and he still felt ashamed.

'You are devoted to your brother,' said the stranger.

'Yes. Everything I do is for him, though he doesn't know it. I have been shaping the history especially to magnify his name.'

'Don't forget what I told you when we first spoke: your name will shine as greatly as his.'

'I don't think of that.'

'No, but it may give you comfort to think that others do, and are working to make sure it comes about.'

'Others? There are others besides you, sir?'

'A legion. And it will come to happen, have no fear about that. But before I go, let me ask you again: do you understand how it might be necessary for one man to die so that many can live?'

'No, I don't understand it, but I accept it. If it is God's will, I accept it, even if it's impossible to understand. The story doesn't say whether Abraham and Isaac understood what they had to do, but they didn't hesitate to do it.'

'Remember your words,' said the angel. 'We shall talk again in Jerusalem.'

He kissed Christ on the brow before leaving with the scrolls.

Jesus Rides into Jerusalem

Next day, Jesus and his followers prepared to leave for Jerusalem. Word had spread that he was coming, and many people came to see him and welcome him on his way to the city, because his fame was now so widespread. The priests and the scribes, of course, had been aware of him for some time, and they didn't know how best to react. It was a difficult matter for them: should they endorse him and hope to share his popularity, at the cost of not knowing what he would do next? Or should they condemn him, and risk offending the people who supported him in such numbers?

They resolved to watch closely, and to test him whenever they saw the chance.

Jesus and his disciples had reached Bethphage, near a place called the Mount of Olives, when he told them to stop and rest. He sent two of the disciples to find a beast for him to ride on, because he was tired. All they could find was the foal of a donkey, and when the owner heard who it was for, he refused any payment.

The disciples spread their cloaks on the donkey and Jesus rode it into Jerusalem. The streets were thronged with people curious to see him, or eager to welcome him. Christ was among the crowd, watching everything, and he saw how one or two people had cut palm branches to wave; he was already composing the account of the scene in his mind. Jesus was calm and unaffected by the clamour, and acknowledged all the questions that people called out without answering any of them:

'Are you going to preach here, master?'

'Are you going to heal?'

'What are you going to do, Lord?'

'Will you go to the temple?'

'Have you come to speak to the priests?'

'Are you going to fight the Romans?'

'Master, will you heal my son?'

The disciples cleared a way to the house where he was going to stay, and presently the crowd dispersed.

The Priests Test Jesus

But the priests were determined to test him, and soon the chance came. They tried three times, and each time Jesus baffled them.

The first test came when they said to him 'You preach, you heal, you cast out devils – now, by whose authority do you do these things? Who gave you permission to go about stirring up excitement like this?'

'I'll tell you,' he said, 'if you'll give me an answer to this question: did John's authority to baptise come from heaven, or from earth?'

They didn't know how to answer him. They withdrew a little way and discussed it. 'If we say it came from heaven,' they said, 'he'll say "In that case, why didn't you believe in it?" But if we say it was of human origin, the crowd will be angry with us. John's a great prophet as far as they're concerned.'

So they had to tell him 'We find it hard to decide. We can't answer you.'

'In that case,' he said, 'you'll have to do without an answer from me.'

The next test they put him to concerned that perennial difficulty, taxes.

They said 'Teacher, you're an honest man, we can all see that. No one doubts your sincerity or your impartiality; you show no favours, and you don't try to ingratiate yourself with anyone. So we're sure you'll give us a truthful answer when we ask you: is it lawful to pay taxes?'

They meant lawful according to the law of Moses, and they hoped they would trick him into saying something that would get him into trouble with the Romans.

But he said 'Show me one of those coins you pay taxes with.'

Someone handed him a coin, and he looked at it and said 'There's a picture on here. Whose picture is this? What's the name underneath it?'

'It's Caesar's, of course,' they said.

'Well, there's your answer. If this is Caesar's, give it back to him. Give God the things that are God's.'

The third time they tried to trap him involved a capital offence. The scribes and the Pharisees happened to be dealing with the case of a woman who was caught committing adultery. They thought that they could force Jesus into calling for her to be stoned, which was the punishment authorised by their law, and hoped that this would cause trouble for him.

They found him near the temple wall. The Pharisees and scribes took the woman out and stood her in front of him, and said 'Teacher, this woman has committed adultery – she was caught in the act! Moses commands us to stone such a woman to death. What do you say? Should we do it?'

Jesus was sitting on a rock, leaning down and writing with his finger in the dust. He took no notice of them.

'Teacher, what should we do?' they said again. 'Should we stone her, as Moses says?'

He still said nothing, and went on writing in the dust.

'We don't know what to do!' they went on. 'You can tell us. We're sure you can find a solution. Should she be stoned? What do you think?'

Jesus looked up and brushed the dirt off his hands.

'If there's one of you who has never committed a sin, he can throw the first stone,' he said.

Then he bent down again and wrote some more.

One by one the scribes and the Pharisees went away, muttering. Jesus was left alone with the woman.

Finally he stood up and said 'Where have they gone? Has no one condemned you, after all?'

'No, sir, no one,' she said.

'Well, you'd better go too, then,' he said. 'I'm not going to condemn you. But don't sin any more.'

Christ heard about this from the disciple who was his informant. As soon as he was told about it, he hurried to the spot to see what it was that Jesus had written in the dust. The wind had blown his words away, and there was nothing to see on the ground, but nearby someone had daubed the words KING JESUS on the temple wall in mud. It had dried in the sunlight, and Christ brushed it off quickly in case it got his brother into trouble.

Jesus Becomes Angry
with the Pharisees

Soon after that, something provoked Jesus into anger with the Pharisees. He had been watching how they behaved, how they dealt with ordinary people, how they assumed airs of importance. A questioner had asked him whether people should do as the Pharisees did, and Jesus said:

'They teach with the authority of Moses, don't they? And you know what the law of Moses says? Listen to what the scribes and the Pharisees say, and if they agree with the law of Moses, obey them. But do as they say – don't do as they do.

'Because they're hypocrites, every one of them. Look at the way they vaunt themselves up! They love to sit in the place of honour at a banquet, they love to sit in prominent positions in the synagogue, they love to be greeted with respectful words in the marketplace. They preen themselves on the correctness of their costume, while exaggerating every detail to draw attention to their piety. They encourage superstition and they ignore genuine faith, while all the time they're fawning over prominent citizens and boasting of the importance of their powerful friends. Haven't I told you many times how wrong it is to think that the higher you are among men, the closer you are to God?

'You scribes and Pharisees, if you're listening – be damned to you. You take endless scruples over the tiniest matters of the law, while you let the great things like justice and mercy and faith go unnoticed and forgotten. You strain the gnats out of your wine, but you ignore the camel standing in it.

'Damn the lot of you – hypocrites that you are. You preach modesty and abstinence, while indulging in the costliest luxuries; you're like a man who offers his guests wine from a golden cup, having polished the outside while neglecting the inside, so it's full of dirt and slime.

'Damn you each and every one. You're like a tomb covered in whitewash, a handsome structure, gleaming and spotless – but what's on the inside? Bones and rags and all kinds of filth.

'You snakes, you brood of vipers! You've

persecuted the best and the most innocent, you've hounded the wisest and the most righteous to death. How in the world do you think you're going to escape being sent to hell?

'Jerusalem, Jerusalem – what an unhappy city you are. They come to you, the prophets, and you stone them to death. I wish I could gather all your children together as a hen gathers her brood under her wings! But will you let me? No, not a chance. See how sad you make those who love you!'

News of this angry speech spread quickly, and Christ had to work hard to keep up with the reports of his brother's words. And more and more frequently he saw the words scrawled on walls, or scratched into the bark of trees: KING JESUS.

Jesus and the Money-changers

The next thing to happen didn't only involve words. In the temple there were many activities connected with buying and selling: for example, doves and cattle and sheep were offered for sale to those who wanted to make a sacrifice. But as people came to the temple from many places both near and far away, some of them had money different from the local coinage, and there were money-changers there too, ready to calculate the exchange rate and sell them the money to buy doves with. One day Jesus went into the temple and, provoked by his growing anger against the scribes and the priests, lost his patience with all this mercantile activity and began to upset the tables of the money-changers and the animal-sellers.

He flung them this way and that, and took a whip and drove the animals out, shouting 'This should be a house of prayer, but look at it now! It's a den of robbers! Take your money and your buying and selling elsewhere, and leave this place to God and his people!'

The temple guards came running to try and restore order, but the people were too excited to listen to them, and some were scrambling to gather up the coins that were rolling all over the floor before the money-changers could save them. In the confusion the officials missed Jesus, and failed to arrest him.

The Priests Discuss
What to Do about Jesus

Of course, the priests and officials of the temple were aware of all this, and they gathered at the house of the high priest Caiaphas to discuss how to respond.

'We shall have to put him out of action one way or another,' said one.

'Arrest him? Kill him? Exile him somewhere?'

'But he's so popular. If we move against him, the people won't stand for it.'

'The people are fickle. They can be moved this way and that.'

'Well, we're not succeeding in moving them. They're entirely for Jesus.'

'That can change in a moment, with the right provocation . . . '

'I still don't see what he's done wrong.'

'What? Provoking a riot in the temple? Rousing the people to an unhealthy state of excitement? If you don't see it, the Romans certainly will.'

'I don't understand what he wants. If we offered him a high position here, would he accept that and keep quiet?'

'He preaches the coming of the Kingdom of God. I don't think he could be bought off with a salary and a comfortable office.'

'He's a man of great integrity – say what else you like, you must grant him that.'

'Have you seen that slogan they're scrawling everywhere – King Jesus?'

'There's something in that. If we could persuade the Romans that he's a threat to their order . . . '

'Is he a Zealot, do you think? Is that what motivates him?'

'They're bound to be aware of him. We really must move before they do.'

'We can't do anything during the festival.'

'We need an agent in his camp. If we could find out what he was planning next . . . '

'Impossible. His followers are fanatics – they'd never give him away.'

'It can't go on. We'll have to do something soon. He's had the initiative for too long.'

Caiaphas let everyone speak and listened to everything, and his mind was troubled.

Christ and his Informant

Christ was staying at an inn at the edge of the city. That evening he ate with his informant, who told him about the incident in the temple. Christ had already heard rumours about what had happened, and he was eager to get the facts clear, so he made notes on his tablet as they ate.

'Jesus seems more and more angry,' he said. 'Do you know why that is? Has he spoken about it to any of you?'

'No, but Peter is sure Jesus is in danger, and he's worried that the master will be arrested before the Kingdom comes. What would happen then, with Jesus in prison? Would all the gates be opened, and all the bars flung down? That's the most likely thing. But Peter's anxious, no doubt about it.'

'Is Jesus anxious too, do you think?'

'He hasn't said so. But everyone's jumpy. We don't know what the Romans will do, for one thing. And the crowds – they're all for Jesus now, but there's an edge to it. You can tell. They're over-excited. They want the Kingdom right away, and if . . . '

The man hesitated.

'If what?' said Christ. 'If the Kingdom doesn't come, is that what you were going to say?'

'Of course not. There's no doubt about the Kingdom. But a business like the temple this morning . . . There are times when I wish we were back in Galilee.'

'How are the other disciples taking it?'

'Nervous, jumpy, like I say. If the master wasn't so angry right now we'd all be calmer. It's as if he's spoiling for a fight.'

'But he's said that if someone hits us, we should turn the other cheek.'

'He also said he'd come not to bring peace, but a sword.'

'When did he say that?'

'That was in Capernaum, not long after Matthew joined us. Jesus was telling us what to do when we went out to preach. He said "Don't think I've come to bring peace to the earth. I haven't come to bring peace, but a sword. I've come to set a man against his father, and a daughter against her mother, and a daughter-in-law against her mother-in-law; and your enemies will be members of your own household."'

Christ wrote it down just as the apostle told him.

'That sounds exactly like the sort of thing he'd come out with,' he said. 'Did he say anything else?'

'He said "Those who find their life will lose it, and those who lose their life for my sake will find it." There's some of us thinking of those words again now.'

The Stranger Tells Christ
What Part He Must Play

The man said goodbye, and hastened back to his companions. Christ went to his room to transcribe the words on to a scroll, and then he knelt down, intending to pray for strength to withstand the test that was to come.

But he hadn't been praying for long before there came a knock on the door. Knowing who it was, he got up and let the angel in.

The angel greeted him with a kiss.

'I'm ready, sir,' said Christ. 'Is it tonight?'

'We have a little time to talk first. Sit, and take some wine.'

Christ poured some wine for himself, and for the angel, too, knowing that angels had eaten and drunk with Abraham and Sarah.

'Sir, since I am not going to be here for long,' said Christ, 'will you answer a question I've put to you more than once, and tell me who you are and where you come from?'

'I thought we had come to trust each other, you and I?'

'I have given my life into your hands. All I ask is a little knowledge in return.'

'This is not the first occasion on which your faith has failed.'

'If you know about the other occasion, sir, you will know how much I lamented it. I would give anything to live that night again. But haven't I done faithfully everything you've asked of me? Haven't I written a true record of my brother's life and words? And now, haven't I assented to the role you told me of last time we spoke? I am ready to play the part of Isaac. I'm ready to give my life for the Kingdom, and atone for the time when my faith was needed, and when it failed. Sir, let me plead with you: I beg you, tell me more. Otherwise I shall go out of my life in darkness.'

'I told you that this task would be difficult. The part of Isaac is easy; it's the part of Abraham that is hard. You are not to die. You are to give Jesus to the authorities. He is the one who will die.'

Christ was astounded.

'Betray my brother? When I love him as I do?

I could never do that! Sir, that's too hard! I beg you, don't ask this of me!'

In his distraction, Christ got up and beat his hands together and struck his head. Then he fell to the floor and clasped the angel's knees.

'Let me die in his place, I beg you!' he cried. 'We look similar – no one will know – he can continue his work! What am I doing except keeping a record? Anyone could do that! My informant is a good and honest man – he could write it – he would be well placed to continue the history I've begun – you don't need me to live! All my life I have been trying to serve my brother, and now, when I thought I could do him the greatest service of all by dying in his place, are you going to rob me of it by making me betray him instead? Don't bring me to this! I can't do it, I can't; let it pass me by!'

The angel stroked Christ's hair.

'Sit up now,' he said, 'and I shall tell you a little of what's been hidden.'

Christ wiped his tears and tried to compose himself.

'The truth of everything I say is already known to you,' the stranger began. 'You have said much of it to Jesus in your own words. You told him that people needed miracles and signs; you told him of the importance of dramatic events in persuading them to believe. He didn't listen, because he thought that the Kingdom was coming so soon that no persuasion would be necessary. And again, you urged him to accept the existence of what we have agreed to call the church. He scoffed at the idea. But he was wrong, and you were right. Without miracles, without a church, without a scripture, the power of his words and his deeds will be like water poured into the sand. It dampens the sand for a moment, and then the sun comes and dries it, and after a minute there's no sign that it's ever been there. Even the history that you've begun to write so meticulously, with such diligence and care for the truth, even that will be scattered like dry leaves and forgotten. In another generation the name of Jesus will mean nothing, and neither will the name Christ. How many healers and exorcists and preachers are there walking the roads of Galilee and Judea? Dozens and dozens. Every one will be forgotten, and so will Jesus. Unless—'

'But the Kingdom,' said Christ, 'the Kingdom will come!'

'No,' said the angel, 'there will be no Kingdom in this world. You were right about that as well.'

'I never denied the Kingdom!'

'You did. When you described the church, you spoke as if the Kingdom would not come about without it. And you were right.'

'No, no! I said that if God wanted to, he could bring the Kingdom about just by lifting a finger.'

'But God does not want to. God wants the church to be an image of the Kingdom. Perfection does not belong here; we can only have an image of perfection. Jesus, in his purity, is asking too much of people. We know they're not perfect, as he wishes them to be; we have to adjust ourselves to what they are. You see, the true Kingdom would blind human beings like the sun, but they need an image of it all the same. And that is what the church will be. My dear Christ,' the stranger went on, leaning forward, 'human life is difficult; there are profundities and compromises and mysteries that look to the innocent eye like betrayal. Let the wise men of the church bear those burdens, because there are plenty of other burdens for the faithful to carry. There are children to educate, there are the sick to nurse, there are the hungry to feed.

The body of the faithful will do all these things, fearlessly, selflessly, ceaselessly, and it will do more, because there are other needs as well. There is the desire for beauty and music and art; and that is a hunger that is a double blessing to assuage, because the things that satisfy it are not consumed, but go on to nourish everyone who hungers for them, again and again for ever. The church you describe will inspire all these things, and provide them in full measure. And there is the noble passion for knowledge and inquiry, for philosophy, for the most royal study of the nature and mystery of divinity itself. Under the guidance and protection of the church, all these human needs from the most common and physical to the most rare and spiritual will be satisfied again and again, and every covenant will be fulfilled. The church will not be the Kingdom, because the Kingdom is not of this world; but it will be a foreshadowing of the Kingdom, and the one sure way to reach it.

'But only – only – if at the centre of it is the ever-living presence of a man who is both a man and more than a man, a man who is also God and the word of God, a man who dies and is brought to life again. Without that, the church will wither and perish, an empty husk, like every other human structure that lives for a moment and then dies and blows away.'

'What are you saying? What is this? Brought to life again?'

'If he does not come to life again, then nothing will be true. If he doesn't rise from his grave, the faith of countless millions yet unborn will die in the womb, and that is a grave from which nothing will rise. I told you how truth is not history, and comes from outside time, and comes into the darkness like a light. This is that truth. It's a truth that will make everything true. It's a light that will lighten the world.'

'But will it happen?'

'Such stubbornness! Such hardness of heart! Yes, it will happen, if you believe in it.'

'But you know how weak my faith is! I couldn't even . . . You know what I couldn't do.'

'We are discussing truth, not history,' the angel reminded him. 'You may live history, but you must write truth.'

'It's in history that I want to see him rise again.'

'Then believe.'

'And if I can't?'

'Then think of an orphan child, lost and cold and starving. Think of a sick man, racked with pain and fear. Think of a dying woman terrified by the coming darkness. There will be hands reaching out to comfort them and feed them and warm them, there will be voices of kindness and reassurance, there will be soft beds and sweet hymns and consolation and joy. All those kindly hands and sweet voices will do their work so willingly because they know that one man died and rose again, and that this truth is enough to cancel out all the evil in the world.'

'Even if it never happened.'

The angel said nothing.

Christ waited for a response, but none came. So he said 'I can see now. It's better that one man should die than that all these good things should never come about. That's what you're saying. If I'd known it would come to this, I wonder if I'd ever have listened to you in the first place. And I'm not surprised that you left it till now before making it clear. You've caught me in a net so that I'm tangled like a gladiator and I can't fight my way out.'

Still the angel said nothing.

Christ went on 'And why me? Why must it be my hand that betrays him? It's not as if he's hard to find. It's not as if no one in Jerusalem knows what he looks like. It's not as if there are no greedy scum who wouldn't give him away for a handful of coins. Why must I do it?'

'Do you remember what Abraham said when he was commanded to sacrifice his son?' said the angel then.

Christ was silent.

'He said nothing,' he said finally.

'And do you remember what happened when he lifted the knife?'

'An angel told him not to harm the boy. And then he saw the ram caught in the thicket.'

The angel stood up to leave.

'Take your time, my dear Christ,' he said. 'Consider everything. When you're ready, come to the house of Caiaphas, the high priest.'

Christ at the Pool of Bethesda

Christ meant to stay in his room and think about the ram in the thicket: did the angel mean that something would happen at the last minute to save his brother? What else could he have meant?

But the room was small and stuffy, and Christ needed fresh air. He wrapped his cloak around himself and went out into the streets. He walked towards the temple, and then away again; he walked towards the Damascus gate, and then turned to one side, whether left or right he didn't know; and presently he found himself at the pool of Bethesda. This was a place where invalids of every kind came in the hope of being healed. The pool was surrounded by a colonnade under which some of the sick slept all night, though they were supposed to come only during the hours of daylight.

Christ made his way quietly under the colonnade and sat on the steps that led down to the pool. The moon was nearly full, but clouds covered the sky, and Christ could not see much apart from the pale

stone and the dark water. He hadn't been there for
more than a minute when he heard a shuffling sound,
and turned in alarm to see something coming
towards him: a man whose legs were paralysed pulling
himself laboriously over the stone pavement.

Christ got up, ready to move away, but the
man said 'Wait, sir, wait for me.'

Christ sat down again. He wanted to be alone,
but he remembered the angel's description of the
good work that would be done by that church
they both wanted to see; could he possibly turn
away from this poor man? Or could the beggar in
some unimaginable way be the ram that would be
sacrificed instead of Jesus?

'How can I help you?' Christ said quietly.

'Just stay and talk to me for a minute or two,
sir. That's all I want.'

The crippled man pulled himself up next to
Christ and lay there breathing heavily.

'How long have you been waiting for a cure?'
said Christ.

'Twelve years, sir.'

'Will no one help you to the water? Shall I help
you now?'

'No good now, sir. What happens is that an

angel comes every so often and stirs the water up, and the first one in the pool afterwards gets cured. I can't move so quickly, as you may have noticed.'

'How do you live? What do you eat? Have you got friends or a family to look after you?'

'There's some people who come along some-times and give us a bit of food.'

'Why do they do that? Who are they?'

'I don't know who they are. They do it because . . . I don't know why they do it. Maybe they're just good.'

'Don't be stupid,' said another voice in the darkness. 'No one's good. It's not natural to be good. They do it so's other people will think more highly of them. They wouldn't do it otherwise.'

'You don't know nothing,' said a third voice from under the colonnade. 'People can earn high opinions in quicker ways than doing good. They do it because they're frightened.'

'Frightened of what?' said the second voice.

'Frightened of hell, you blind fool. They think they can buy their way out of it by doing good.'

'Doesn't matter why they do it,' said the lame man, 'as long as they do it. Anyway, some people are just good.'

'Some people are just soft, like you, you worm,' said the third voice. 'Why's no one helped you down to the water in twelve years? Eh? Because you're filthy, that's why. You stink, like we all do. They'll throw a bit of bread your way, but they won't touch you. That's how good they are. You know what real charity would be? It wouldn't be bread. They don't miss bread. They can buy more bread whenever they want. Real charity would be a pretty young whore coming down here and giving us a good time for nothing. Can you imagine a sweet-faced girl with skin like silk coming and laying herself down in my arms, with my sores oozing pus all over her and stinking like a dung-heap? If you can imagine that, you can imagine real goodness. I'm damned if I can. I could live a thousand years and never see goodness like that.'

'Because it wouldn't be goodness,' said the blind man. 'It'd be wickedness and fornication, and she'd be punished and so would you.'

'There's old Sarah,' said the lame man. 'She come down here last week. She does it for nothing.'

'Because she's mad and full of drink,' said the leper. 'Mad enough to lie with you, anyway. But even she wouldn't lie with me.'

'Even a dead whore wouldn't lie with you, you filthy leper,' said the blind man. 'She'd get out of her grave and crawl away in her bones sooner than that.'

'You tell me what goodness is, then,' said the leper.

'You want to know what goodness is? I'll tell you what goodness is. Goodness would be to take a sharp knife and go round the city by night and cut the throats of all the rich men, and their wives and their children, and their servants too, and every living thing in their houses. That'd be an act of supreme goodness.'

'You can't say that'd be good,' said the lame man. 'That'd be murder, rich men or not. That's forbidden. You know it is.'

'You're ignorant. You don't know the scriptures. When King Sennacherib was besieging Jerusalem the angel of the Lord came down in the night and slew one hundred and eighty-five thousand of his soldiers while they was all asleep. That was a good deed. It's righteous and holy to slay the oppressor – always has been. You tell me if we poor people aren't oppressed by the rich. If I was a rich man I'd have servants to fetch and carry for me, I'd have a wife to lie with me, I'd have children to honour my name, I'd have harpists and singers to make sweet music for me, I'd have stewards to look after my money and manage my fields and livestock, I'd have every convenient thing to make life easy for a blind man. The high priest would call on me, I'd be praised in the synagogues, I'd be respected all through Judea, blind or not.'

'And would you give charity to a poor cripple by the pool of Bethesda?' said the lame man.

'No, I wouldn't. Not a penny. And why not? Because I'd still be blind, and I wouldn't be able to see you, and if anyone tried to tell me about you, I wouldn't listen. Because I'd be rich. You wouldn't matter to me.'

'Well, you'd deserve to have your throat cut, then,' said the leper.

'That's what I'm saying, isn't it?'

Christ said 'There's a man called Jesus. A holy man, a healer. If he came here—'

'Waste of time,' said the leper. 'There's a dozen or more beggars who come here every day, pretending to be cripples, hiring themselves out to the holy men. A couple of drachmas and they'll swear they've been crippled or blind for years and then stage a bloody miraculous recovery. Holy men? Healers? Don't make me laugh.'

'But this man is different,' said Christ.

'I remember him,' said the blind man. 'Jesus. He come here on the sabbath, like a fool. The priests wouldn't let him heal anyone on the sabbath. He should've known that.'

'But he did heal someone,' said the lame man. 'Old Hiram. You remember that. He told him to take up his bed and walk.'

'Bloody rubbish,' said the blind man. 'Hiram went as far as the temple gate, then he lay down and went on begging. Old Sarah told me. He said what was the use of taking his living away? Begging was the only thing he knew how to do. You and your blether about goodness,' he said, turning to Christ, 'where's the goodness in throwing an old man out into the street without a trade, without a home, without a penny? Eh? That Jesus is asking too much of people.'

'But he *was* good,' said the lame man. 'I don't care what you say. You could feel it, you could see it in his eyes.'

'I never saw it,' said the blind man.

Christ said to the lame man 'And what do you think goodness is?'

'Just a little human companionship, sir. A poor man has got little to enjoy in this life, and a cripple even less. The touch of a kindly hand is worth gold to me, sir. If you was to embrace me, sir, just put your arms around me for a moment and kiss me, I'd treasure that, sir. That would be real goodness.'

The man stank. The smell of faeces, urine, vomit, and years of accumulated filth rose from him in a cloud. Christ leant down and tried to embrace him, and had to turn away, and retched, and tried again. There was a moment of clumsiness as the lame man's arms tried to embrace him in return, and then the smell became too much, and Christ had to kiss him very quickly and then push him away and stand up.

A short laugh came from the darkness under the colonnade.

Christ hurried outside and away, breathing the cold air deeply, and only when he had passed the great tower at the corner of the temple complex did he discover that during their clumsy embrace the lame man had stolen the purse that hung from his girdle.

He sat down trembling in a corner of the wall and wept for himself, for the money he'd lost, for the three men by the pool of Bethesda, for his brother Jesus, for the prostitute with the cancer, for all the poor people in the world, for his mother and father, for his own childhood, when it had been so easy to be good. Things could not go on like this.

When he had recovered he went to meet the angel at the house of Caiaphas, but he could not stop trembling.

Caiaphas

When Christ arrived he found the angel waiting in the courtyard, and the two of them were shown into the high priest's presence at once. They found him rising from prayer. He had dismissed all his advisers, saying that he needed to ponder their words; but he greeted the angel as if he were a valued counsellor.

'This is the man,' said the angel, indicating Christ.

'It is very good of you to come. May I offer you some refreshment?' said Caiaphas.

But Christ and the angel refused.

'Better so, perhaps,' said Caiaphas. 'This is an unhappy business. I do not want to know your name. Your friend will have told you what we require. The guards who will arrest Jesus have been drafted in from elsewhere, and don't know what he looks like, so we need someone who can point him out. You are willing to do this?'

'Yes,' said Christ. 'But why have you had to draft in extra guards?'

'There is considerable disagreement – I am being very frank – not only in our council, but among the people in general, and the guards are not immune to this. Those who have seen and heard Jesus are excited, volatile, unstable; some love him and some deplore him. I have to send a squad I can rely on not to argue among themselves. This is a very delicate situation.'

'Have you yourself seen and heard him?' said Christ.

'Unfortunately I haven't had the opportunity. Naturally, I've heard full reports of his words and deeds. If times were easier I would greatly enjoy meeting him and discussing matters of common interest. But I have to maintain a very difficult balance. My overriding concern is to keep the body of the faithful together. There are factions that would like to split away entirely and join with the Zealots; there are others that would like nothing better than for me to rally all the Jews in open defiance of the Romans; there are others that urge me to maintain good relations with the governor, on the grounds that our greatest duty is to preserve the peace and the lives of our people. I have to satisfy as many of these demands as I can, while not alienating those who have to be disappointed, and above all, as I say, keeping some kind of unity. It's hard to get the balance right. But the Lord has placed this burden on my shoulders, and I must bear it as best I can.'

'What will the Romans do to Jesus?'

'I . . . ' Caiaphas spread his hands wide. 'They will do what they will do. It wouldn't be long before they picked him up themselves in any case. And that's another of our problems; if the religious authorities don't take steps to deal with this man, it will seem as if we're supporting him, and that will put all the Jews in danger. I must look after my people. The governor, alas, is a brutal man. If I could save this man Jesus, if I could perform a miracle and transport him in a moment to Babylon or to Athens, I would do it at once. But we are constrained by circumstances. There is nothing else I can do.'

Christ bowed his head. He could see that Caiaphas was a good and honest man, and that his position was impossible.

The high priest turned away and picked up a little bag of money.

'Now you must let me pay you for your trouble,' he said.

And Christ remembered that his purse had been stolen, and that he owed money for the rent of his room. At the same time, he felt ashamed to take this money from Caiaphas. He knew that the angel saw he was hesitating, and he turned to explain.

'My purse was—'

But the angel held up a hand in understanding. 'No need to explain,' he said. 'Take the money. It's offered in perfect honesty.'

So Christ took it, and felt sick again.

Caiaphas said goodbye to the two of them, and summoned the captain of the guard.

Jesus in the Garden at Gethsemane

Now all that evening Jesus had been sitting with his disciples and talking with them, but at midnight he said 'I'm going out. Peter, James, John, come with me; the rest of you can stay and sleep.'

They left the others and walked towards the nearest gate in the city wall.

Peter said 'Master, be careful tonight. There's a rumour that they're reinforcing the temple guards. And the governor's looking for an excuse to crack down – everyone's talking about it.'

'Why would they do that?'

'Things like this,' said John, pointing to the mud-daubed words KING JESUS on the nearest wall.

'Did you write that there?' said Jesus.

'Of course not.'

'Well, it doesn't concern you, then. Ignore it.'

John knew that it concerned them all, but he said nothing. He stayed to brush the words off and then hurried after the others.

Jesus went across the valley to a garden on the slopes of the Mount of Olives.

'Wait here,' he said. 'Keep watch. Let me know if anyone comes.'

They sat down under an olive tree and wrapped their cloaks around them, because the night was cold. Jesus went apart a little way and knelt down.

'You're not listening,' he whispered. 'I've been speaking to you all my life and all I've heard back is silence. Where are you? Are you out there among the stars? Is that it? Busy making another world, perhaps, because you're sick of this one? You've gone away, haven't you, you've abandoned us.

'You're making a liar out of me, you realise that. I don't want to tell lies. I try to tell the truth. But I tell them you're a loving father watching over them all, and you're not; you're blind as well as deaf, as far as I can tell. You can't see, or you just don't want to look? Which is it?

'No answer. Not interested.

'If you were listening, you'd know what I meant by truth. I'm not one of these logic-choppers, these fastidious philosophers, with their scented Greek rubbish about a pure world of spiritual forms where everything is perfect, and which is the only place where the real truth is, unlike this filthy material world which is corrupt and gross and full of untruth and imperfection . . . Have you heard them? Stupid question. You're not interested in slander either.

'And slander's what it is; you made this world, and it's lovely, every inch of it. When I think of the things I've loved I find myself choking with happiness, or maybe sorrow, I don't know; and every one of them has been something in this world that you made. If anyone can smell frying fish on an evening by the lake, or feel a cool breeze on a hot day, or see a little animal trying to run around and tumbling over and getting up again, or kiss a pair of soft and willing lips, if anyone can feel those things and still maintain they're nothing but crude imperfect copies of something much better in another world, they are slandering you, Lord, as surely as words mean anything at all. But then they don't think words do mean anything; they're just tokens to play sophisticated games with. Truth is this, and truth is that, and what is truth anyway, and on and on they go, these bloodless phantoms.

'The psalm says "The fool has said in his heart,

There is no God." Well, I understand that fool. You treated him as you're treating me, didn't you? If that makes me a fool, I'm one with all the fools you made. I love that fool, even if you don't. The poor sod whispered to you night after night, and heard nothing in response. Even Job, for all the trouble he had, got an answer from you. But the fool and I might as well be talking into an empty pot, except that even an empty pot makes a sound like the wind, if you hold it over your ear. That's an answer of sorts.

'Is that what you're saying to me? That when I hear the wind, I hear your voice? When I look at the stars I see your writing, or in the bark of a tree, or the ripples on the sand at the edge of the water? Lovely things, yes, all of them, no doubt about that, but why did you make them so hard to read? Who can translate them for us? You conceal yourself in enigmas and riddles. Can I believe that the Lord God would behave like one of those philosophers and say things in order to baffle and confuse? No, I can't believe it. Why do you treat your people like this? The God who made water to be clear and sweet and fresh wouldn't fill it with mud before giving it to his children to drink. So, what's the answer? These things are full of your words, and we just have to persevere till we can read them? Or they're blank and meaningless? Which is it?

'No answer, naturally. Listen to that silence. Not a breath of wind; the little insects scratching away in the grasses; Peter snoring over there under the olives; a dog barking on some farm out behind me in the hills; an owl down in the valley; and the infinite silence under it all. You're not in the sounds, are you. There might be some help in that. I love those little insects. That's a good dog out there; he's trustworthy; he'd die to look after the farm. The owl is beautiful and cares for her young. Even Peter's full of kindness, for all the noise and the bluster. If I thought you were in those sounds, I could love you with all my heart, even if those were the only sounds you made. But you're in the silence. You say nothing.

'God, is there any difference between saying that and saying you're not there at all? I can imagine some philosophical smartarse of a priest in years to come pulling the wool over his poor followers' eyes: "God's great absence is, of course, the very sign of his presence", or some such drivel.

The people will hear his words, and think how clever he is to say such things, and they'll try and believe it; and they'll go home puzzled and hungry, because it makes no sense at all. That priest is worse than the fool in the psalm, who at least is an honest man. When the fool prays to you and gets no answer, he decides that God's great absence means he's not bloody well there.

'What am I going to tell the people tomorrow, and the day after, and the day after that? Am I going to go on telling them things I can't believe? My heart will grow weary of it; my belly will churn with sickness; my mouth will be full of ash and my throat will burn with gall. There'll come a day when I'll say to some poor leper that his sins are forgiven and his sores will heal and he'll say "But they're as bad as they ever were. Where is this healing you promised?"

'And the Kingdom . . .

'Have I been deluding myself as well as everyone else? What have I been doing, telling them that it's going to come, that there are people alive now who will see the coming of God's Kingdom? I can see us waiting, and waiting, and waiting . . . Was my brother right when he talked of this great organisation, this church of his that was going to serve as the vehicle for the Kingdom on earth? No, he was wrong, he was wrong. My whole heart and mind and body revolted against that. They still do.

'Because I can see just what would happen if that kind of thing came about. The devil would rub his hands with glee. As soon as men who believe they're doing God's will get hold of power, whether it's in a household or a village or in Jerusalem or in Rome itself, the devil enters into them. It isn't long before they start drawing up lists of punishments for all kinds of innocent activities, sentencing people to be flogged or stoned in the name of God for wearing this or eating that or believing the other. And the privileged ones will build great palaces and temples to strut around in, and levy taxes on the poor to pay for their luxuries; and they'll start keeping the very scriptures secret, saying there are some truths too holy to be revealed to the ordinary people, so that only the priests' interpretation will be allowed, and they'll torture and kill anyone who wants to make the word of God clear and plain to all; and with every day that passes they'll become more and more fearful, because the more power they have the less they'll trust anyone, so they'll have spies and betrayals and denunciations and secret tribunals, and put the poor harmless heretics they flush out to horrible public deaths, to terrify the rest into obedience.

'And from time to time, to distract the people from their miseries and fire them with anger against someone else, the governors of this church will declare that such-and-such a nation or such-and-such a people is evil and ought to be destroyed, and they'll gather great armies and set off to kill and burn and loot and rape and plunder, and they'll raise their standard over the smoking ruins of what was once a fair and prosperous land and declare that God's Kingdom is so much the larger and more magnificent as a result.

'But any priest who wants to indulge his secret appetites, his greed, his lust, his cruelty, will find himself like a wolf in a field of lambs where the shepherd is bound and gagged and blinded. No one will even think of questioning the rightness of what this holy man does in private; and his little victims will cry to heaven for pity, and their tears will wet his hands, and he'll wipe them on his robe and press them together piously and cast his eyes upwards and the people will say what a fine thing it is to have such a holy man as priest, how well he takes care of the children . . .

'And where will you be? Will you look down and strike these blaspheming serpents with a thunderbolt? Will you strike the governors off their thrones and smash their palaces to rubble?

'To ask the question and wait for the answer is to know that there will be no answer.

'Lord, if I thought you were listening, I'd pray for this above all: that any church set up in your name should remain poor, and powerless, and modest. That it should wield no authority except that of love. That it should never cast anyone out. That it should own no property and make no laws. That it should not condemn, but only forgive. That it should be not like a palace with marble walls and polished floors, and guards standing at the door, but like a tree with its roots deep in the soil, that shelters every kind of bird and beast and gives blossom in the spring and shade in the hot sun and fruit in the season, and in time gives up its good sound wood for the carpenter; but that sheds many thousands of seeds so that new trees can grow in its place. Does the tree say to the sparrow "Get out, you don't belong here?" Does the tree say to the hungry man "This fruit is not for you?" Does the tree test the loyalty of the beasts before it allows them into the shade?

'This is all I can do now, whisper into the silence. How much longer will I even feel like doing that? You're not there. You've never heard me. I'd do better to talk to a tree, to talk to a dog, an owl, a little grasshopper. They'll always be there. I'm with the fool in the psalm. You thought we could get on without you; no – you didn't care whether we got on without you or not. You just got up and left. So that's what we're doing, we're getting on. I'm part of the world, and I love every grain of sand and blade of grass and drop of blood in it. There might as well not be anything else, because these things are enough to gladden the heart and calm the spirit; and we know they delight the body. Body and spirit . . . is there a difference? Where does one end and the other begin? Aren't they the same thing?

'From time to time we'll remember you, like a grandfather who was loved once, but who has died, and we'll tell stories about you; and we'll feed the lambs and reap the corn and press the wine, and sit under the tree in the cool of the evening, and welcome the stranger and look after the children, and nurse the sick and comfort the dying, and then lie down when our time comes, without a pang, without a fear, and go back to the earth.

'And let the silence talk to itself . . . '

Jesus stopped. There was nothing else he wanted to say.

The Arrest of Jesus

But a little distance away John was sitting up and rubbing his eyes, and then he kicked Peter awake and pointed down into the valley; and then got to his feet and hurried up to where Jesus was still kneeling by himself.

'Master,' he said, 'I'm sorry, forgive me, I don't want to disturb you, but there are men with torches coming up the path from the city.'

Jesus took John's hand and stood up.

'You could get away, master,' John said. 'Peter's got a sword. We can hold them off – tell them we haven't seen you.'

'No,' said Jesus. 'I don't want any fighting.'

And he walked down the path towards the other disciples, and told Peter to put his sword away.

As they came up the path in the torchlight Christ said to the captain of the guards 'I'll embrace him, and you'll know who it is.'

When they came close to Jesus and the other three, Christ went up to his brother and kissed him.

'You?' said Jesus.

Christ wanted to speak, but he was shoved aside as the guards moved past him. He was soon lost among the crowd of curious onlookers who had heard rumours of what was going to happen, and come along to watch.

Seeing Jesus under arrest, the people thought that he'd betrayed their trust in him; that he was just another religious deceiver, like so many others, and that everything he'd told them had been false. They began to shout and jeer, and they might even have attacked and lynched him there and then, if the guards had not held them off; Peter tried to draw his sword again, but Jesus saw him and shook his head.

Peter said 'Master! We're with you! We won't leave you! Wherever they take you, I'll come too!'

The guards marched Jesus off down the path, and Peter hastened after them. They took him through the city gate and along to the house of the high priest. Peter had to wait in the courtyard outside, where he joined the servants and the guards around the brazier they'd lit to keep themselves warm, for it was a cold night.

Jesus before the Council

Inside the house, Caiaphas had called together an emergency council of the chief priests and the elders and the scribes. This was unusual, because Jewish law normally prohibited courts from sitting at night, but the circumstances were urgent; if they were going to deal with Jesus the priests would have to do it before the festival began.

Jesus was brought before this council, and they began to question him. Some of the priests who had lost to him in argument were eager for a reason to hand him over to the Romans, and they had summoned witnesses in the hope of convicting him. However, they hadn't coached the witnesses well enough, and several of them contradicted one another; for example, one said 'I heard him say he could destroy the temple, and build another in three days.'

'No! That wasn't him!' said another. 'That was one of his followers.'

'But Jesus didn't deny it!'

'It was him. I heard him say it myself.'

Not all the priests were sure that was reason enough to condemn him.

Finally Caiaphas said 'Well, Jesus, what have you got to say? What's your answer to these charges?'

Jesus said nothing.

'And what about this other charge of blasphemy? That you claim to be the son of God? The Messiah?'

'That's what you say,' said Jesus.

'Well, it's what your followers say,' said Caiaphas. 'Don't you bear any responsibility for that?'

'I have asked them not to. But even if I had said that, it would not be blasphemy, as you well know.'

Jesus was right, and Caiaphas and the priests knew it. Strictly speaking, blasphemy consisted of cursing the name of God, and Jesus had never done that.

'Then what about this claim to be king of the Jews? We see it everywhere daubed on the walls. What have you to say to that?'

Jesus said nothing.

'Silence is no answer,' said Caiaphas.

Jesus smiled.

'Jesus, we're trying very hard to be fair to you,' the high priest went on. 'It seems to us that you've gone out of your way to provoke trouble, not only with us, but with the Romans. And these are difficult times. We have to protect our people. Can't you see that? Don't you understand the danger you're putting everyone in?'

Jesus still said nothing.

Caiaphas turned to the priests and scribes, saying 'I'm sorry to say that we have very little choice. We shall have to take this man to the governor in the morning. Of course, we shall pray that he is merciful.'

Peter

While this was happening inside the high priest's house, the courtyard was crowded with people clustering around the brazier for warmth, and talking with anxious excitement about the arrest of Jesus, and what was likely to happen next. Peter was there among them, and at one point a servant girl looked at him and said 'You were with that Jesus, weren't you? I saw you with him yesterday.'

'No,' said Peter. 'He's nothing to do with me.'

A little later someone else said to his companions 'This man was one of Jesus's followers. He was in the temple with him when he upset the money-changers' tables.'

'Not me,' said Peter. 'You must be mistaken.'

And just before dawn a third person, hearing Peter make some remark, said 'You're one of them, aren't you? I can tell by your accent. You're a Galilean, like him.'

'I don't know what you're talking about,' said Peter.

Just then a cock crew. Until that moment the world had seemed to be holding its breath, as if time itself were suspended during the hours of darkness; but soon the daylight would come, and with it the full desolation would break in. Peter felt that, and he went outside and wept bitterly.

Jesus and Pilate

After Christ had betrayed his brother to the soldiers, he went by himself to pray. He hoped that the angel would come back to him, because he felt he had to talk about what he'd done and what might happen next; and he badly wanted to explain about the money.

He prayed, but he couldn't sleep, so at first light he went to the high priest's house, where he heard about the Galilean who had denied being one of Jesus's followers, and who had wept at the cock-crow. Even in the middle of his tension and distress, Christ made a note of that.

But he was restless and agitated still, and joined the crowd that had gathered to see what the verdict on Jesus would be.

Presently a rumour began to spread: they were taking Jesus to the Roman governor. And soon afterwards the doors of the high priest's house opened, and a troop of temple guards came out, bringing Jesus with them, his hands bound behind him. The guards had to protect him from the people, who only a few days ago had welcomed him with cheers and shouts of joy; now they were yelling at him, shaking their fists, and spitting.

Christ followed as they made their way to the governor's palace. The governor at the time was Pontius Pilate, a brutal man much given to handing out cruel punishments. There was another prisoner awaiting sentence, a political terrorist and murderer called Barabbas, and it was almost certain that he was going to be crucified.

Christ remembered the ram caught in the thicket.

When the guards reached the governor's palace, they dragged Jesus inside and flung him down at Pilate's feet. Caiaphas had come to press the charges against Jesus, and Pilate listened while he spoke.

'You will have seen, sir, the daubings on the walls – "King Jesus". This is the man responsible. He has caused chaos in the temple, he has excited the mob, and we are conscious of the danger of civil disorder, so—'

'You hear that?' said Pilate to Jesus. 'I've seen

those filthy daubings. So that was you, was it? You claim to be the king of the Jews?'

'You say that,' said Jesus.

'Did he speak to you in this insolent way?' Pilate asked Caiaphas.

'Constantly, sir.'

Pilate told the guards to set Jesus on his feet.

'I'll ask you again,' he said, 'and I expect some politeness this time. Do you claim to be the king of the Jews?'

Jesus said nothing.

Pilate knocked him down, and said 'You hear all these charges they lay against you? You think we're going to put up with this kind of thing? You think we're stupid, to allow agitators to go around causing trouble and urging the people to riot, or worse? We're responsible for keeping the peace here, if you hadn't noticed. And I will not put up with political disturbance from any direction. I'll stamp that out at once, make no mistake. Well? What have you got to say, King Jesus?'

Again Jesus said nothing, so Pilate told the guards to beat him. By this time they could hear the shouts of the crowd outside, and both the priests and the Romans feared a riot.

'What are they shouting about?' demanded Pilate. 'Do they want this man released?'

Now there was a custom that at the time of Passover, one prisoner of the people's choice would be given his freedom; and some of the priests, in order to agitate the crowd and make sure Jesus didn't escape with his life, had gone among the people urging them to plead for the life of Barabbas.

One of Pilate's officers said 'Not this man, sir. They want you to free Barabbas.'

'That murderer? Why?'

'He is popular, sir. You would please them greatly by letting him go.'

Pilate went out on to his balcony and spoke to the crowd.

'You want Barabbas?' he said.

They all cried 'Yes! Barabbas!'

'Very well, he can go free. Now clear the court-yard. Go about your business.'

He came back into the room, and said 'That means there's a spare cross. You hear that, Jesus?'

'Sir,' said Caiaphas, 'if it would be possible to consider, for example, a sentence of exile—'

'Take him away and crucify him,' said Pilate.

'Put a sign on the cross saying who he claims to be – the king of the Jews. That'll teach you people to think about rebellion and rioting.'

'Sir, could the sign read "*He says* he is king of the Jews?" Just in case, you know—'

'I've said what I've said. Don't push your luck, Caiaphas.'

'No, of course not, sir. Thank you, sir.'

'Take him away then. Flog him first, and then nail him up.'

The Crucifixion

Christ, among the crowd, had wanted to shout
'No!' when Pilate asked if they wanted Barabbas
freed, but he hadn't dared; and he felt his failure
to do so like yet another blow at his heart. There
was not much time now. He searched up and down
among the people, looking for the angel, but saw
him nowhere, and finally, on seeing a stir by the
gates of the governor's mansion, followed the crowd
to see the Roman guards take Jesus to the place
of execution.

He didn't see any of the disciples among the
crowd, but there were some women there whom
he recognised. One of them was the wife of
Zebedee, the mother of James and John, another
was the woman from Magdala, of whom Jesus was
particularly fond, and the third, to his great
surprise, was his own mother. He hung back; he
wanted nothing less, at that moment, than for
her to see him. He watched from a little way off
as they went with the crowd through the city to

the place called Golgotha, where criminals were usually crucified.

Two men were already hanging on crosses there, having been convicted of theft. The Roman soldiers knew their business; it was not long before Jesus was hanging in place beside them. Christ remained with the crowd until it began to thin, which it did before very long: once the victim was nailed to the cross there was not much to see until the soldiers broke his legs to hasten his death, which might not happen for many hours.

The disciples had vanished altogether. Christ went in search of the man who was his informant, in order to find out what they intended to do next, but he found that the man had left the house where he was staying, and the host had no idea where he had gone. Of course, there was no sign of the angel, the stranger, and Christ couldn't ask after him, because he still had no name to call him by.

From time to time, and always reluctantly, he went back to the place of execution, but found no change there. The three women were sitting close by the crosses. Christ took great care not to be seen by any of them.

Late in the afternoon, word got around that

the Roman soldiers had decided to hasten the deaths of the three men. Christ hurried to the scene, sick and fearful, to find the crowd so thick he couldn't see what was happening, but he heard the blows as the last man's legs were smashed, and the satisfied sigh of the crowd, and a high gasping cry from the victim. Some women began to wail. Christ walked away very carefully, as lightly as he could, trying to make no impression on the earth.

The Burial

One of the members of the Sanhedrin was a man from the town of Arimathea, whose name was Joseph. Despite his membership of the council, he was not one of those who'd condemned Jesus; on the contrary, he admired him and was greatly interested in what he'd had to say about the coming Kingdom. Knowing that the Passover was imminent, he went to Pilate and asked for the body.

'Why? What's the hurry?'

'We would like to bury Jesus decently before the sabbath, sir. It's our custom.'

'I'm surprised you bother. The man was nothing but a rabble-rouser. I hope you've all learned a lesson. Take him, if you want him.'

Joseph and a colleague from the Sanhedrin called Nicodemus, another sympathiser, took the body down from the cross with some help from the grieving women. They had it carried to a garden nearby, where Joseph had had a tomb made for himself. The tomb was formed like a cave, and the entrance was closed by a stone that rolled in a groove. Joseph and the others wrapped the body of Jesus in a linen cloth, with spices to keep it from corruption, and closed the tomb in time for the sabbath.

There was still no sign of the disciples.

The Stranger in the Garden

Christ spent the next day alone in the room he had rented, alternately praying and weeping and trying to write down what had happened, or as much of it as he knew. He was afraid of more things than he could count. He didn't feel like eating or drinking, and he couldn't sleep. The money Caiaphas had given him troubled him more and more, until he thought he would go mad from shame, so he paid the landlord what he owed and gave the rest to the first beggar he saw in the street. Still he felt no better.

When evening fell he went to the garden where Joseph had laid Jesus in the tomb, and sat near the grave among the shadows. Presently he became aware that the stranger was sitting next to him.

'I have been busy elsewhere,' said the stranger.

'Yes,' said Christ bitterly, 'going to and fro in the earth, and walking up and down in it.'

'I know this is hard for you. But I am not Satan. The first part of our work is nearly accomplished.'

'And where was the ram caught in the thicket? You let me believe that something would happen to prevent the worst. And nothing happened, and the worst came.'

'You let yourself believe it, and your belief let the great oblation run its course. Thanks to what you did, all kinds of good will come.'

'So he will rise from the dead?'

'Undoubtedly.'

'When?'

'Always.'

Christ shook his head in irritated bewilderment.

'Always?' he said. 'What does that mean?'

'It means that the miracle will never be forgotten, its goodness will never be exhausted, its truth will last from generation to generation.'

'Ah, truth again. Would that be the truth that is different from history?'

'The truth that irradiates history, in your own beautiful phrase. The truth that waters history as a gardener waters his plants. The truth that lights history as a lantern banishes the shadows.'

'I don't think Jesus would have recognised that sort of truth.'

'Which is precisely why we need you to embody it. You are the missing part of Jesus. Without you, his death will be no more than one among thousands of other public executions. But with you, the way is opened for that light of truth to strike in on the darkness of history; the blessed rain will fall on the parched earth. Jesus and Christ together will be the miracle. So many holy things will flower from this!'

They were speaking very quietly, and the garden itself was quiet. But then Christ heard a low rumble, as of stone rolling on stone.

'What's happening?' he said.

'The next part of the miracle. Be calm, dear Christ. All shall be well. Jesus wanted a state of things that no human being could have borne for long. People are capable of great things, but only when great circumstances call on them. They can't live at that pitch all the time, and most circumstances are not great. In daily life people are tempted by comfort and peace; they are a little lazy, a little greedy, a little cowardly, a little lustful, a little vain, a little irritable, a little envious. They are not good for much, but we have to deal with them as they are. Among other things, they're credulous; so they like mysteries, and they adore miracles. But you know this well; you said this to Jesus some time ago. As usual, you were right, and as usual, he didn't listen.'

By the tomb, some figures were moving. It was a cloudy night, and the moon, which was just past the full, was hidden; but there was enough light to see three or four figures carrying something heavy between them away from the tomb.

'What are they doing?' said Christ.

'The work of God.'

'That is Jesus's body!'

'Whatever you see, it is necessary.'

'Are you going to pretend he is risen?'

'He will be risen.'

'How? By means of a trick? This is contemptible. Oh, that I fell for this! Oh, I am damned! Oh, my brother! What have I done?'

And he fell down and wept. The stranger laid his hands on Christ's head.

'Weep,' he said, 'and comfort will come to you.'

Christ remained where he was, and the stranger continued:

'Now I must tell you about the Holy Spirit. He is the one who will fill the disciples, and in time to come more and more of the faithful, with the conviction of the living Jesus. Jesus could not be with people for ever, but the Holy Spirit can, and will. It was necessary for Jesus to die so that the Spirit could descend to this world, and descend he will, with your help. In the days to come you will see the transforming power of the Spirit. The disciples, those weak and troubled men, will become like lions. What the living Jesus could not do, the dead and risen Jesus will bring about by the power of the Holy Spirit, not only in the disciples but in everyone who hears and believes.'

'Then why do you need me? If the Spirit is so all-powerful, what help can I possibly give?'

'The Spirit is inward and invisible. Men and women need a sign that is outward and visible, and then they will believe. You have been scornful lately when I have spoken of truth, dear Christ; you should not be. It will be truth that strikes into their minds and hearts in the ages to come, the truth of God, that comes from beyond time. But it needs a window to be opened so it can shine through into the world of time, and you are that window.'

Christ gathered himself and got to his feet,

and said 'I understand. I shall play my part. But I do so with a bitter conscience and a heavy heart.'

'Of course. It's natural. But you have a great part to play still; when the records of this time and of Jesus's life are written, your account will be of enormous value. You will be able to determine how these events are remembered right up until the ending of the world. You will—'

'Stop, stop. Enough. I want to hear no more for now. I am very tired and unhappy. I shall come back here on the morning after the sabbath, and do whatever I have to do.'

Mary from Magdala at the Tomb

After the crucifixion Peter, John, James and the other disciples had gathered in a house not far from Joseph's garden, where they sat like men bereft of their senses, stunned and silent. The execution of Jesus had come upon them like a thunderbolt out of a blue sky; of all things, they had not expected that. It was no less a shock than if the foundations of the earth had shifted under their feet.

As for the women who had gathered at the foot of the cross and helped Joseph take down the body, they had wept and prayed until they could weep no more. Mary the mother of Jesus had seen him into the grave, and soon she would return to Nazareth. The woman from Magdala, who was also called Mary, was going to remain in Jerusalem for a little while.

Very early on the morning after the sabbath, Mary the Magdalene went to the garden where the tomb was, taking some spices in case any more were needed to preserve the body. It was still dark.

After the burial she had seen Joseph and Nicodemus roll the stone into place over the tomb, and she was surprised to see, in the half-light, the stone rolled back and the tomb yawning open. She wondered if she had come to the right grave, and she looked inside fearfully.

There she saw the linen cloth wrapped up and empty, but no body.

She ran out and hurried to the house where the disciples were staying, and said to Peter and John 'The master's tomb is empty! I've just been there, and the stone is rolled back, and the body is gone!'

She told them everything she had seen. A woman's testimony being of little value, Peter and John hastened to the garden to see for themselves. John ran faster and got to the grave first, and looked inside to see the linen cloth lying empty; and then Peter pushed past him and went inside, and found the cloth just as Mary had described, with the cloth that had wrapped Jesus's head not lying with the rest, but apart by itself.

John said 'Have the Romans taken him away?'

'Why would they do that?' said Peter. 'Pilate released his body. They wouldn't be interested.'

'What else can have happened?'

'He might not have been dead when they took him down. Only fainted, like. Then he might have woken up . . . '

'But how could he have rolled the stone away from inside? His legs were broken. He couldn't move.'

They could make no sense of it at all. They left the tomb and hurried back to tell the other disciples.

Mary the Magdalene, who had remained outside, was weeping. But then through her tears she saw a man close by, and took him for the gardener.

'Why are you weeping?' he said.

'They've taken my master's body away, and I don't know where he is. Sir, if you know where they've taken him, please tell me, I beg you, and I'll bring him back here and look after him properly.'

Then the man said 'Mary.'

She was startled, and she looked at him more closely. It was still not quite light, and her eyes were sore, but surely this was Jesus, alive.

'Master!' she cried, and then moved to embrace him.

But Christ stepped back and said 'No, don't

touch me now. I shan't be here for long. Go to the disciples and tell them what you've seen. Tell them I shall ascend soon and go to my father, to God. To my God and your God.'

Mary ran and told the disciples what she had seen, and what Christ had said to her.

'It was him!' she told them. 'Truly! Jesus was alive, and he spoke to me!'

They were half-sceptical, but Peter and John were more ready than the others to believe her.

'She told us how the cloth was laid out in the tomb, and we went and we saw it, just as she said. If she says he's alive – well, that would explain it! It would explain everything!'

They passed that day in a state of half-hopeful wonderment. They went again and again to the garden where the tomb was, but saw no more there.

The Road to Emmaus

Later that day some of the disciples set out to go
to a village called Emmaus, about two hours' walk
away from Jerusalem, to tell the news to some
friends who lived there. Christ's informant had set
off back to Galilee, and was not among them. As
they walked along the road they fell into conversation with a man who was travelling the same
way. This too was Christ.

'You seem agitated,' said the traveller. 'What
were you all discussing with such passion?'

'You haven't heard what happened in Jerusalem?'
said a disciple called Cleopas.

'No. Tell me.'

'You must be the only man in Judea not to have
heard about it. We're friends of Jesus of Nazareth,
the great prophet, the great teacher. He angered
the priests in the temple, and they handed him
over to the Romans, and they crucified him. And
he was buried. That was three days ago. And then
this morning we heard he'd been seen alive!'

Their talk was only of that. They didn't look closely at Christ, because they were too excited and bewildered still; but by the time they came to the village night had fallen, and they invited him to stay and eat with them.

He accepted the invitation, and went into the house of their friend, where he was made welcome. When they were sitting down to eat, the disciple Cleopas, who was sitting directly opposite him, stopped what he was saying, took hold of the lamp and raised it close to Christ's face.

'Master?' he said.

In the flickering lamplight the others stared in amazement. Truly, this man looked so like Jesus, and yet he was not the same; but surely death would change him, so he was bound to be a little different; and yet the resemblance was so close. They were struck almost dumb.

But one man called Thomas said 'If you're really Jesus, show us the marks in your hands and your feet.'

Christ's hands were unmarked, of course. They could all see them as he held the bread. But before he could speak, another man intervened and said:

'If the master's risen from the dead, of course

all his wounds would be healed! We've seen him walk – we know his broken legs are mended. He'd be made perfect again, so his other scars are gone as well. Who can doubt that?'

'But his legs weren't broken!' said another. 'I heard it from one of the women! He died when a soldier stuck a spear into his side!'

'I never heard that,' said another. 'I heard they broke his legs first of all, before they did the other two. They always break their legs . . . '

And they turned to Christ, full of doubt and confusion.

Christ said 'Those who see no evidence, and still have faith, are the blessed ones. I am the word of God. I existed before time. I was in the beginning with God, and soon I shall go back to him, but I came down into time and into life so that you should see the light and the truth, and testify to them. I shall leave you a sign, and here it is: just as the bread has to be broken before you can eat it, and the wine has to be poured before you can drink, so I had to die in one life before I rose again in another. Remember me as often as you eat and drink. Now I must return to my father, who is in heaven.'

They all wanted to touch him, but he stood back and blessed them all, and then he left.

After that, Christ took care to keep out of the way. He watched from a distance as the disciples, fired by the energy of their hope and excitement, became transformed just as the stranger had promised: as if a holy spirit had entered them. They travelled and preached, they won converts to this new faith in a risen Jesus, they even managed some healing miracles, or at least things happened that could be reported as miracles. They were full of passion and zeal.

And as time passed, Christ began to hear the story changing little by little. It began with Jesus's name. At first he was Jesus, simply; but then he began to be called Jesus the Messiah, or Jesus the Christ; and later still it was simply Christ. Christ was the word of God, the light of the world. Christ had been crucified. Christ had risen from the dead. Somehow, his death would be a great redemption, or a great atonement. People were happy to believe that, even though it was hard to explain.

The story developed in other ways too. The account of the resurrection was greatly enhanced when it began to be reported that after Thomas asked to see the wounds, Jesus (or Christ) had shown them, and let Thomas lay his finger in them to settle his doubts. That was vivid and unforgettable, but if the story said that, it couldn't also say that the Romans had broken his legs, as they did with almost every other victim of crucifixion; for if one kind of wound had remained in his flesh, so would another, and a man with broken legs would not have been able to stand in the garden or walk to Emmaus. So whatever had really happened, the story came to say that he died from the thrust of a Roman spear, his bones remaining unbroken. Thus the stories began to weave themselves together.

Christ himself, of course, had made so little mark on the world that no one confused him with Jesus, because it was so easy to forget that there had been two of them. Christ felt his own self gradually dwindling away as the Christ of speculation began to grow in importance and majesty. Soon the story about Christ began to extend both forwards and backwards in time – forwards to the end of the world, and backwards even before that birth in a stable: Christ was the son of Mary, that was undeniable, but he was also the son of God, an eternal and almighty being, perfect God and perfect man, begotten before all worlds, reigning at the right hand of his Father in heaven.

The Net-Maker

Then the stranger visited him for the last time. Christ was living under another name in a town on the sea-coast, a place where Jesus had never been. He had married, and he was working as a maker of nets.

As often before, the stranger came at night. He knocked at the door just as Christ and his wife were sitting down to their evening meal.

'Martha, who is that?' said Christ. 'Go and see.'

Martha opened the door, and the stranger came in, carrying a heavy bag.

'So,' said Christ. 'What trouble have you brought me this time?'

'Such a welcome! This is your work, all the scrolls you gave to me. I have had them diligently copied, and it is time you had them back and began putting the story in order. And this is your wife?'

'Martha,' said Christ, 'this is the man I told you about. But he has never told me his name.'

'Please sit with us and share our food,' said Martha.

'I shall do that with pleasure. That little ritual you invented,' the stranger said as Christ broke the bread, 'has been a great success. Who would have thought that inviting Jews to eat flesh and drink blood would be so popular?'

Christ pushed the bread away. 'That is not what I told them to do,' he said.

'But it's what the followers of Jesus are doing, Jews and Gentiles both. Your instructions were too subtle, my friend. People will leap to the most lurid meaning they can find, even if it's one the author never intended.'

'As you explained on another occasion, you think very little of people.'

'I see them as they are. You too used to have a realistic idea of their capabilities and limitations. Are you becoming more like your brother as time goes past?'

'He knew them well, and he wasn't deceived, but he loved them.'

'Indeed he did,' said the stranger, helping himself to the bread, 'and his love is the most precious thing imaginable. That is why we must

guard it so carefully. The vessel that will carry
the precious love and teaching of Jesus Christ to the
ages of the future is the church, and the church
must guard that love and teaching night and day,
to keep it pure and not let it be corrupted by
misunderstanding. It would be unfortunate, for
example, if people came to read some of his sayings
as a call to political action; as we know, they are
nothing of the sort. Instead we should emphasise
the spiritual nature of his message. We need to
make our position hard to argue with, my dear
Christ, and by talking of the spirit we do just that.
Spirituality is something we are well equipped to
discuss.'

'I have no taste for that sort of talk any more,'
said Christ. 'You had better take your scrolls away
with you. Let someone else tell the story.'

'The story will be told many times. We shall
make sure of that. In the years to come we shall sort
out the helpful versions from the unhelpful. But
we have spoken of these things before.'

'Yes, and I'm sick of it. Your words are smooth,
but your thoughts are coarse. And you have become
coarser with your success. When you first spoke
to me you were more subtle. I begin to see now

what it is, this story you and I and my brother have been playing out. However it ends, it will be a tragedy. His vision could never come to pass; and the vision that will come to pass is not his.'

'You talk of my vision and his vision; but if it were *your* vision it would have all the merit of truth as well as—'

'I know what your truth means,' said Christ.

'Of course you do. But which is better,' said the stranger, breaking off some more bread, 'to aim for absolute purity and fail altogether, or to compromise and succeed a little?'

Christ felt sick for a moment, but he couldn't remember why. Martha slipped her hand into her husband's to steady him.

But as Christ sat and watched the stranger eating his bread and pouring himself more wine, he couldn't help thinking of the story of Jesus, and how he could improve it. For example, there could be some miraculous sign to welcome the birth: a star, an angel. And the childhood of Jesus might be studded with charming little wonder-tales of boyish mischief leavened by magic, which could nevertheless be interpreted as signs of greater miracles to come. Then there were matters of more profound narrative consequence. If Jesus had known about his execution in advance, and told his disciples that it was going to come about, and gone to meet it willingly, it would give the crucifixion a far more resonant meaning, and one that would open depths of mystery for wise men to explore and ponder and explain in the times to come. And the birth, again: if the child born in the stable had been not just a human child, but the very incarnation of God himself, how much more memorable and moving the story would be! And how much more profound the death that crowned it!

There were a hundred details that could add verisimilitude. He knew, with a pang that blended guilt and pleasure, that he had already made some of them up.

'I leave it in your hands,' said the stranger, brushing the breadcrumbs off his own as he stood up from the table. 'I shall not come to you again.'

And without another word he turned to leave.

When he had gone Martha said 'You still didn't ask his name.'

'I don't want to know his name. How deluded I was! How can I ever have thought he was an angel? He has the look of a prosperous dealer in dried fruit or carpets. I don't want to think about him ever again. Martha, I'm tormented; everything he says is true, and yet I feel sick when I think of it. The body of the faithful, the church, as he calls it, will do every kind of good, I hope so, I believe so, I must believe so, and yet I fear it'll do terrible things as well in its zeal and self-righteousness . . . Under its authority, Jesus will be distorted and lied about and compromised and betrayed over and over again. A body of the faithful? It was a body of the faithful that decided for a dozen good reasons to hand him over to the Romans. And here am I, my hands red with blood and shame and wet with tears, longing to begin telling the story of Jesus, and not just for the sake of making a record of what happened: I want to play with it; I want to give it a better shape; I want to knot the details together neatly to make patterns and show correspondences, and if they weren't there in life, I want to put them there in the story, for no other reason than to make a better story. The stranger would have called it letting truth into history. Jesus would have called it lying. He wanted perfection; he asked too much of people

. . . But this is the tragedy: without the story, there will be no church, and without the church, Jesus will be forgotten . . . Oh, Martha, I don't know what I should do.'

'You should eat your supper,' said Martha.

But when they turned back to the table the bread was all gone, and the wine-jar was empty.

Afterword

Some writers – apparently William Golding was one – are firmly of the opinion that there is a correct way to read their books, and they argue strongly with readers who, they think, have got them wrong. My view is exactly the opposite. Readers may interpret my work in any way they please, and people do. Some readers, indeed, have seen things – connections and patterns and implications – I had no idea were there. If such phenomena reflect well on me, of course, I claim to have put them there on purpose.

The problem with *my* telling people what I think such-and-such a story means is that my interpretation seems to have some extra authority, which shuts down debate: if the author himself has said it means X, then it can't mean Y. Believing as I do in the democracy of reading, I don't like the sort of totalitarian silence that descends when there is one authoritative reading of any text.

So in general I prefer not to discuss the meaning

of my work. But *The Good Man Jesus and the Scoundrel Christ* is different from the sort of books I've published before. Its protagonist belongs not just to me but to the history and the culture of the past 2,000 years, and the story about him is not just any story but the foundation story of the Christian religion. It is too important to too many people for me to take my usual line. This time I have to say something about what I've done with this story, and explain, so to speak, where I'm coming from.

§

Christianity formed my mind. I wasn't an unusually pious child, but I did firmly believe in the God I was told about, and I did believe everything I said in the Apostles' Creed every Sunday. I didn't question it for a moment; I assumed it to be true in the way I assumed there to be an equator and lines of latitude and longitude, which I could see on the map but never actually on the ground or on the water. I had crossed the equator four times by the age of nine, each time at sea, and each time the event was celebrated with a jolly ceremony, involving sailors dressed up as King Neptune and people being ducked into the swimming pool.

So I knew that grown-ups behaved as if the equator certainly existed, although you couldn't actually see it; and they did so in serious ways as well as comical ones, because the ships I was on were navigated according to these invisible lines. Grown-ups believed that the equator existed, as did the lines of latitude and longitude, and by acting on this belief they brought me safely to land. Why should I doubt them when they told me that God existed (though you couldn't see Him either), that various improbable events had taken place in the life of Jesus, and that I would go to heaven if I believed it all and was a good boy? I believed every word of it.

A further reason for its hold on me was that Christianity was transmitted to us in those days in the language of the King James Bible, the Book of Common Prayer, and Hymns Ancient and Modern. I was always susceptible to the music of language; it was the rhythms of Kipling's *Just-So Stories* that taught me to read, and I was never daunted by words I didn't understand as long as I could pronounce them. Indeed, singing or intoning or simply whispering words I didn't understand was a sensuous delight. I was perfectly comfortable with not understanding much of what I heard in church: 'In the beginning was the Word, and the Word was with God, and the Word was God' meant little, but resonated greatly; the line 'Lo, he abhors not the Virgin's womb' from the carol 'O come, all ye faithful' was utterly mysterious to me, but delightful to sing.

In fact, the traditions and the language of Christianity are so deeply embedded in my memory, in my nerves and my muscles, that not even a surgical operation could remove them.

However, memories are not enough to sustain a faith. It was in my teenage years that believing finally became impossible; after I'd learned a little science, the meaning of creation in six days and conception by means of the Holy Ghost had to be understood metaphorically rather than literally, and once that was done, the miracles vanished and only God himself was left. Although I carried on a fairly anguished one-sided conversation with Him for some time, the silence on His part was complete.

Nowadays I'm as sure as I can be that there is nothing in that God-shaped space. I'm a thoroughgoing materialist. I think that matter is quite extraordinary and wonderful and mysterious enough, without adding something called spirit to it; in fact any talk about *the spiritual* makes me feel a little uneasy. When I hear such utterances as 'My spiritual journey', or 'I'm spiritual but not religious', or 'So-and-so is a deeply spiritual person', or even phrases of a thoroughly respectable Platonic kind such as 'the eternal reality of a supreme goodness', my reaction is a visceral one. I pull back almost physically. I feel not so much puzzlement as vertigo, as if I'm leaning out over a void. There is just nothing there.

Consequently, the immense and complicated structures of Christian theology seem to me like the epicycles of Ptolemaic astronomy – preposterously elaborated methods of explaining away a basic mistake. When astronomers realised that the planets went round the sun, not the earth, the glorious simplicity of the truth blew away the epicycles like so many cobwebs: everything worked perfectly without them.

And as soon as you realise that God doesn't exist, the same sort of thing happens to all those doctrines such as atonement, the immaculate conception of the Blessed Virgin Mary, original sin, the Trinity, justification by faith, prevenient grace, and so on. Cobwebs, dusty bits of rag, frail scraps of faded cloth: they hide nothing, they decorate nothing, and for me they mean nothing.

'But look at the good work the churches have done!' I hear. 'Look at the hospitals, the orphanages, the schools! And look further, at the architecture, the art and music they have sponsored and inspired!'

Yes, and all those things are good, and we are better off for their existence. They go some way towards mitigating the evils the churches have done too: the Crusades, the witch-hunts, the heretic-burnings, the narrow fanatical zeal that comes so swiftly and naturally to some individuals in positions of power when faith gives them an excuse, the sexual abuse of children that seems to have taken place in some of those very orphanages and schools.

However, the people who use that argument seem to imply that until the church existed no one ever knew how to be good, or create a work of art, or do anything selflessly, and no one could nowadays unless they did it because of their faith. I simply don't believe that.

But as I say, I can't escape my Christian background. And I am a storyteller. We write out of what we are; and I thought it would be interesting to read the gospels again, and to see if I could tell the familiar story from a different angle. So I picked up the Bible. Actually I picked up three: the Authorised Version, the New English Bible, whose publication I remembered causing great excitement when I was a child, and the New Revised Standard Version. Having no Greek, I thought I should at least triangulate between different English versions to get the meaning clear in my mind.

I began there because by far the most important sources for the life of Jesus are the four canonical gospels. The canon of scripture was settled in the fourth century, when the gospels of Matthew, Mark, Luke, and John were chosen by a council of the church to form part of the New Testament. They are the basis for orthodox Christian belief.

But there are many other gospels, some of which have been known for centuries and some of which have been more recently discovered. I thought I should look at them too. One view of these other texts is that of M.R. James, the great writer of ghost stories, who published a translation of various apocryphal gospels in 1924. He wrote:

> People may still be heard to say, 'After all, these Apocryphal Gospels and Acts, as you call them, are just as interesting as the old ones. It was only by accident or caprice that they were not put into the New Testament.' The best answer to such loose talk has always been, and is now, to produce the writings and let them tell their own story. It will very quickly be seen that there is no question of anyone's having excluded them from the New Testament; they have excluded themselves.

In other words, they're just not very good. And it's true: for the most part, the apocryphal gospels in James's selection have nothing like the clarity and force of Matthew, Mark, and Luke, or the poetry of John. They include some remarkable fragments, but also a welter of undistinguished narratives, sayings, exhortations, and fairy tales that make pretty hard reading.

A different view of the value of the 'excluded'

gospels comes from Elaine Pagels, whose book *The Gnostic Gospels* (1979) introduced many readers to the texts that were found at Nag Hammadi in Egypt in 1945. With the knowledge of these new sources (which were, of course, not available to M.R. James) she implies that the excluded texts were left out of the canon for another reason: 'Why were these other writings excluded and banned as "heresy"? What made them so dangerous?'

Some of those other writings are fascinating indeed. But I wasn't interested in heresy and danger at this point so much as in narrative pure and simple, and I particularly wanted to revisit the stories that were known to me as a child, so I returned to Matthew, Mark, Luke, and John.

I considered the gospels purely as stories, and I was struck by how unlike most other narratives they are. They're not biographies, because so much of the subject's life is left out: instead the focus is almost entirely on the last year or two of his life and deeds. They're not novels, with the novel's interest in psychology and feeling and emotional relationships; and furthermore there is no description. What did Jesus look like? We have no idea. There are no landscapes; there is a storm, but apart from that no weather to speak of, and novelists enjoy weather and use it a lot. In their spareness and urgency the gospel narratives resemble folktales and ballads, except that they have a quite different purpose: to tell us what to believe.

The problem is that they seem to tell us to believe contradictory things. John's gospel tells us that Jesus's expulsion of the money-changers from the Temple took place at the beginning of his ministry; the other gospels say that it happened just before his crucifixion. At one point Jesus seems to be telling his listeners to take no thought for the morrow, and at another he condemns those foolish girls who didn't think ahead and bring enough oil for their lamps; one day he blesses the peacemakers, and another he says he has come not to send peace, but a sword.

Of course, the church has had two thousand years to reconcile these contradictions and paradoxes, and there is no shortage of smooth and polished interpretations that make perfect sense, if you have a taste for that sort of thing. I preferred the roughness and mystery of the original. Could it have come from a man working out his own thoughts as he spoke? Could there have been another voice close by, 'correcting' what the first voice said so as to make it conform to an emerging 'line'?

There was something else I wondered about: something that felt like fiction. Most of the gospel narratives describe events at which there were other people present as well as Jesus, who could testify to what had happened. Even strange and unlikely events, such as the Transfiguration, occur in the presence of witnesses. There is always someone who can vouch for the truth of the narrative.

But on two occasions, Jesus is represented as being alone. The first is during the temptation in the wilderness, where he encounters Satan, who tries unsuccessfully to tempt him. How did the gospel writers know what Jesus said and did on that occasion? Logically, they could only know if he told them; but does that feel likely? The Jesus we see elsewhere does not tell stories about himself.

The other occasion is when Jesus and three of the disciples, Peter, James, and John, go to the garden of Gethsemane on the night of his arrest. He tells the disciples to remain where they are while he goes a little way off, a stone's throw away, and prays by himself. We are told the words of his prayer, and the Luke writer even says that his sweat became like great drops of blood falling on the ground: pretty much a close-up view. But in all three accounts, in Matthew, Mark, and Luke, we are told that the disciples fell asleep and Jesus had to wake them up. If none of them were awake, there was no one to witness Jesus's prayer, no one to see those drops of sweat like blood, no one to see the angel who, according to the Luke writer, came down from heaven to give him strength. And there was no time afterwards for Jesus to have told the disciples what went on in those anguished minutes, because he is arrested and taken away almost at once, and they never speak to him again. So again: how do the gospel writers know these things?

Altogether, those two passages felt very like fiction to me. The first is school debating society knockabout and the second is profound and very moving psychological drama, but if they don't even pretend to produce any evidence or name any witnesses, I can only regard them as fiction.

And then there was the problem implicit in the very name Jesus Christ. Jesus and Christ, it seemed to me, were two quite separate beings. There was the man Jesus, whom the Gospels talked about, and there was the other sort of being, Christ, the Messiah, who featured more prominently in the Epistles. In the letters Paul wrote, he uses the term 'Christ' 150 or so times, and 'Jesus' about 30. Paul is clearly much more interested in Christ; by the time he wrote, a generation or so after the crucifixion, the myth was already overtaking the man.

In short it seemed to me that Jesus was a man, obviously a man and no more than a man, but Christ was a fiction. That tied in with what I felt about the other voice 'correcting' the Gospels, and the idea began to intrigue me. Suppose there was not one character, but two: how would the story work then?

Needless to say, the second character – the Christ – could not be God. I can't write about things I don't, at some level, believe in. I'd have to find another way of representing him. At the same time, I wanted this Christ to embody as much as possible of what the church later did to alter, edit, and ignore the words of Jesus, and to benefit from his death and his supposed resurrection.

What happened as I wrote and as the story appeared under my hands was something many writers will recognise: a character began to move, speak, and think independently of my intentions. This Christ developed in a way I hadn't expected, and found himself with a human conscience, tempted and torn and compromised. And in the end what compels him to do what he does is the desire to tell a story, but he no longer thinks that his story will tell the truth; the Stranger has told him that truth is not the same as history. Truth is transcendent, eternal, above the vicissitudes of time and chance, and the job of the storyteller is to alter history, if necessary, so that it serves the cause of that greater truth. The Stranger himself, of course, expresses the view the church would express, if there were such a thing as a single church, and it could intervene in its own history, and it had a voice. I can't help it if from time to time he sounds like the Devil.

The story at the heart of Christianity leads to the cross, but it doesn't end there. The cross has a dramatic visual clarity that accounts for much of its success as a symbol (it's a triumphant piece of what would now be called branding), but no

Christian would claim that the death on the cross was the climax of the Christian story. The climax is the resurrection. That's the part that everything else is leading up to.

And as to that resurrection, there's one supreme piece of narrative tact in all four Gospels. We never see the resurrection itself: we only see the consequences. An account of a dead body coming to life and walking out of a graveyard would be squalid, grotesque, bathetic. The confused, contradictory, almost breathless accounts of what happened on the morning after the Sabbath when one woman, or two, or three, came to the empty tomb are vastly superior as storytelling.

Do I believe them, though? Yes, in the way I believe the account in the *Iliad* of Priam's visit to the tent of Achilles. That is also moving and convincing: when I read it I feel that if that event had happened, it would have happened just like that.

But it's a story, and I think that's all it is. In his book *The Resurrection* (2008), the great Jesus scholar Geza Vermes examines six possible explanations for the empty tomb, finding none of them entirely satisfactory; and concludes that the best way of understanding the event is to think of a 'resurrection in the hearts of men'. If only Christians had been wise enough to leave it at that.

§

And what of Jesus?

I keep thinking of that man who, two thousand years ago, was betrayed and flogged and put to death.

And I imagine this: I imagine a procession of ghostly visitors to Jerusalem in that week before Passover – spirits from the future, ghosts of Pope and priest and prelate and preacher, cardinals and archbishops and elders and patriarchs, in all the panoply and splendour of their rank, the chasubles, the albs, the copes, the pectoral crosses, the jewelled rings, the mitres, the tailored suits and the Cadillacs, the gleaming teeth and the bouffant hair.

And I imagine that each of these ghosts has the power, should he wish to use it, to embrace Jesus, much as Judas did, but for a different purpose: their kiss will transport him magically at once to Alexandria, or Athens, or Baghdad, or Rome, and thus save his life. There would be no terrible death on the cross. Jesus would live on, perhaps to vanish into obscurity, perhaps to add to the extraordinary and wonderful words he had spoken, perhaps even to write a book; but at least alive and safe from that appalling death.

And I imagine each of these ghosts looking at the man as he goes about his angry work, denouncing the money-changers, debating with the scribes and chief priests and lashing them with his wit and his scorn, and getting closer every day to the betrayal and the death that each of the ghosts has known about for so long.

And I imagine the ghosts whispering:

'After all, it's God's will . . .'

'He foretold it himself . . .'

'I can't stand in the way . . .'

'It's a painful and sorrowful thing, no doubt, but after all, three days later . . .'

'The entire current of human history from that day on would be turned aside, and would go in a different direction altogether. Do I dare risk changing what I know for something that might be much worse? Non-believers would say it might be better, of course; but there would be no church, so I cannot believe it would be better. This is too great a responsibility for me to bear . . .'

'My grandeur! The magnificence of my cathedral! The splendour of the music in my choir! It is my duty not to give those things up . . .'

'Looking at it in all, taking an objective view, the church without Jesus is better than Jesus without the church. I shall let him die . . .'

'The poor, the oppressed, and the sick need to know that their God suffered as they do, and understands their pain. The crucifixion is the event that shows them he means it. This testimony to God's honesty has comforted so many unhappy souls – should I casually take that great consolation away?'

'The whole theology of the Passion, of redemption, of sin and sacrifice and atonement, the beautiful meditations on the Sacred Heart and the Five Wounds and the Stations of the Cross – are all these profound spiritual exercises, these majestic intellectual constructions to be wiped out at once? It is too much. Surely God would not want us to suffer their loss . . .'

'Without this death and what came after it,

that little dying child I spoke to in the hospital will have no solace . . .'

They look at the man, they see his rough hands and dirty fingernails, they hear the rasp of his voice, they smell a sweet ointment mingled with the sweat from his body, they see the snap and flash of his eyes as he scoffs at the Pharisees; and any one of the ghosts could reach out and save him from the death that's two days, a day, a few hours away.

And for a thousand reasons, for the very best of reasons as well as the worst, each of the ghosts holds back and turns aside; and proudly or fastidiously, humbly or uneasily, with diplomatic murmurs of regret or with passionate sorrow, they drift away and go back to their own time and the comforts and rituals of the church they know, and abandon the man to his death.

That's the thought-experiment I'd put to every believing Christian: if you could go back in time and save that man from the horrible death by crucifixion, would you or not? And if you think it would be better to let him die, how different are you from Judas?

The Myths Series

Myths are universal and timeless stories that reflect and shape our lives – they explore our desires, our fears, our longings and provide narratives that remind us what it means to be human. *The Myths* series brings together some of the world's finest writers, each of whom has retold a myth in a contemporary and memorable way. Authors in the series include: Alai, Karen Armstrong, Margaret Atwood, AS Byatt, Michel Faber, David Grossman, Milton Hatoum, Natsuo Kirino, Alexander McCall Smith, Tomás Eloy Martínez, Klas Östergren, Victor Pelevin, Ali Smith, Su Tong, Dubravka Ugrešic, Salley Vickers and Jeanette Winterson.